Fear of Purple

DUNCAN GRAY

Published by Ultrabizz

Fear of Purple

ISBN-13: 978-0-9873604-0-3

In this work of fiction, the characters, places and events are either the product of the author's imagination or they are used entirely fictitiously. Any resemblance to actual persons, living or dead, is purely coincidental.

Conditions of Sale

To Maxine for encouraging me to start writing.

Chapter 1

Golakov crouched next to the train track and opened his backpack. He took out two blocks of C4 explosive and pressed them up against the rails, one on each side. His thick meaty hands became slightly sticky and he grinned as he savored the familiar smell of the explosive. He knew what the result of his handiwork would be and was looking forward to seeing the aftermath later that morning.

It was 3.00 AM and he knew he had plenty of time. This section of the train track would not see another train until at least 4.30 AM. He glanced back in the direction of the tunnel entrance where, about fifty meters away he could just make out the red glowing end of Todorova's cigarette. He did not like him much but he had useful skills and could be depended on. Golakov did not have to worry about any unwanted guests from that direction, Todorova would make sure of that.

He glanced down the track in the other direction even though he knew it was extremely unlikely that anyone would approach from that direction. This part of the track was raised above ground along a distance of five hundred meters before going back underground to join Kings Cross Station. The elevated track also had raised concrete side sections which were roughly waist high. Nobody could see him from the four lane roadway below either.

Golakov mentally patted himself on the back. He was pleased with his choice of location for this little surprise that would eliminate the ASIO agent who had dared to stick his nose into his business. It had to look like a random terrorist event and the more dramatic it was, the better. Nobody would believe that all this death and destruction had been carried out just to kill one person.

He busied himself with his task again, attaching the trigger device which was the high-tech equivalent of the RFID scanners found in department store entrances which detect electronic tags attached to unpaid merchandise. This European military version he was using had its sensor coil embedded in a black rubber mat which fitted perfectly between two of the sleepers holding up the rails. He plugged the sensors cable into a black receiver box which he placed into the concave side of the rail and was held in place by two magnets built into the devices housing. Two detonator cables ran from the other end of the box to the two C4 putty blobs.

Golakov admired his workmanship in the dim light provided by the clear night sky. It was a rather simple setup, not rocket science, but he took great pride in doing it anyway. *One last thing to do*, he thought. He took a can of matte black non-conductive spray paint out of his backpack and carefully sprayed the creamy white C4 putty. He waited several seconds for it to dry and then pressed the activation button on the receiver box. A small red light blinked three times to show that it was prearmed. The receiver would only go fully active in five minutes time, a useful safety precaution, not that Golakov doubted his handiwork.

He stood up, picked up his backpack and walked back to where Todorova waited. Neither of them spoke, it was not necessary, they just walked over the embankment and across the park to where they had left the car in the parking area in front of the Sydney Art Gallery.

Jack was walking casually towards Bondi Junction station, enjoying the morning sunshine. It was going to be another beautiful summer day in Sydney. His thoughts drifted back to Bondi Beach. He had already been for a one kilometer jog followed by a dip in the ocean at Bondi Beach, part of his daily fitness routine. To tell the truth, he also enjoyed the excuse to see some of the beautiful women who also used the beach as a morning exercise venue. Those *early birds* were generally in better shape and better looking than the lazier crowd who started filling up the beach from 11:00AM onwards. *Plonkers* was the term some people used to describe the mid-day crowd of beach goers who did not come to swim but rather to plonk themselves down on the sand and soak up sun and admiration from male lurkers who came to ogle the bikinis.

Some woman did actually go swimming and Jack, over a period, had noticed a particular blonde who did some surfing. She usually wore one piece swimsuits or a three-quarter wetsuit when the weather got chilly. She was no plonker and was clearly very fit and looked like she could take care of herself. *Confident and intelligent* was how Jack had summarized her body language. They had smiled at each other in passing but Jack had not yet initiated any flirtatious conversations and neither had she. He did notice that she was not wearing a wedding ring.

'Morning mate!'

'Yeah! And it's a good one,' replied Jack whilst giving a warm smile to the local who had greeted him. People were friendly here in Bondi Junction. Like most cities, different Sydney suburbs each had their own characteristics and reputations. Jack had chosen to buy here because he liked the atmosphere of the place and its location suited his various needs. He could walk to the train station in under ten minutes, drive to the airport in under ten minutes or even take the train to the Airport.

His job often required travel within Australia and as an ASIO agent, the mode of travel would depend on the mission parameters. Jack took the train whenever he could because it was more relaxing than fighting peak morning traffic and he preferred blending in with the crowd. Missions which needed vehicles were done using company vehicles, not the agents personal car.

This morning was nothing special, Jack was going into the office to continue following up on some leads which had been of interest. The job had its ups and downs, some periods were intense and full of action and then when a particular case like that was closed, it was back to the routine of following up on leads to see if any developed into urgent cases.

Jack crossed over Grafton street and walked east toward the station entrance. Morning traffic was going by on Syd Einfield drive and buses were loading and off loading people in front of the station building, filling the air with the distinctive sound of their diesel engines. Jack walked past the bustle of people seeing some familiar faces and just as many unfamiliar ones. Many tourists came to the area to visit the world-famous Bondi Beach. One such unfamiliar face belonged to a man leaning against the wall with his back partially towards Jack. He was staring down intently at his smart-phone while he chewed on a pen.

###

Todorova gazed at the smart-phone he was holding. He was watching a live video feed from a miniature bluetooth camera which was cleverly concealed beneath the touristy *I love Australia* cap he was wearing. He watched Jack approaching from behind, then as Jack drew near he used his thumb to close the app he was using, revealing a web browser screen showing things of interest in the area.

Once Jack had passed, he casually sauntered into the station building and caught up with him at the platform entrance where he pressed a button on the pen he was holding. It was no ordinary pen. It was a British made puffer, popular with MI5 and MI6 agents. From the outside it resembled a cheap pen but internally it was built like a miniature pellet gun and could fire tiny pellets or projectiles about half the size of a grain of rice, with an effective range of three to five meters. These pellets might be tracking devices or could be hollow and laced with a poison or drug to suit a particular requirement. Today it was loaded with a tracking device which was coated with micro barbs.

The tracker hit the back of Jack's jacket, right on the right shoulder blade where its micro barbs got caught in the fiber and stuck. The impact force was so small that it was not noticeable and Todorova could not even see it with his naked eyes. He would have to get within a few centimeters of Jack if he wanted to visually confirm that the tracker had adhered to the jacket. However, it was not necessary to get that close.

Todorova swiped his train ticket through the ticket machine and joined the other people waiting on the platform. He then took out a small device which looked like a regular computer thumb drive and plugged it into the USB port of the smart-phone. Another special purpose phone app opened up and gave visual indication that a tracker device was within the limited range of the scanner which Todorova was now holding. He checked the serial number of the tracker which his scanner had detected. He had to be sure it was the same as the one he had puffed onto Jack. It was *really* unlikely that anyone else was using similar equipment but Todorova was trained to be thorough. Satisfied that the numbers matched, he unplugged the scanner device from his smart-phone and waited for the train. He wanted to be sure that Jack got on the train.

A few minutes later the train arrived and Jack got on board. Todorova was watching from his vantage point a few meters down the platform. Satisfied that Jack was in the carriage, he also boarded the train but he chose the next carriage. He planned to get off at Kings Cross station but if for some reason the train bypassed the station he was going to make his way through the connecting doors to the last carriage where he might get some bruises but it would be a survivable option.

The train pulled out of the station and Todorova glanced around at all the stupid Aussies. He did not care much for the happy attitudes that most of them had. Many looked half asleep despite the fact that it was 8:20 AM already. Probably the result of partying the previous night and too much drinking. Sloppy people, and weak. Others were clearly office workers and worked in the city financial district. They wore dark business suits and looked more serious but they could surely not have progressed beyond middle management or they would never have taken the train to work. There were also a few students on board, probably heading for the University near Central station. They were mostly preoccupied with listening to music on their iPods or chatting away on mobile phones.

His attention went back to a rather pretty young student with prominent breasts. He mentally cupped his hands around them and felt himself harden. *Too bad,* he thought.

Todorova got off the train at Kings Cross and another throng of Aussies climbed aboard. He turned and watched the train depart. The pretty student had not gotten off.

Golakov was walking along the pedestrian walkway which covered the Cahill Expressway next to the Sydney Art Gallery. His stocky build and eastern European appearance made him look like a foreigner in Australia, so he usually played the tourist card. He had a video camera and even did some filming, just like a tourist would.

He was interrupted by the sound of machine-gun fire, but he did not run for cover. Instead he casually took out his mobile phone and answered the call. It was Todorova.

'Breakfast is ready,' he said and hung up.

Golakov casually walked the last few meters to where the paved and grassed walkway overlooked the busy roadway below. He raised the video camera back up and pointed it in the direction of the train which was now making its way along the raised track. He followed with his camera. It would look great on YouTube and he wanted his bosses to be impressed. High definition video would certainly impress them.

Just as the second carriage rolled over the section where the bomb was, the receiver Golakov had placed there detected the presence of the tracker device in the carriage above. In a few micro-seconds it had validated the serial number of the tracker device and sent a current down the connecting wires to the detonators embedded in the C4 explosives. The detonators exploded forcing a high temperature, high pressure shock wave into the C4.

Golakov felt a satisfying thud beneath his feet as the C4 exploded and simultaneously saw a bright flash just as the carriage began to lift into the air. The sound of the explosion reached him a half a second later.

The second carriage continued to rise up into the air until it just cleared the concrete embankment of the overhead track then fell back down on its side, pulling the first and third carriages off the rails as well. The trains momentum carried it forward and the carriages screeched as they scraped along the concrete and steel at sixty kilometers per hour. Three seconds later the lead carriage slammed into the front of the tunnel entrance and jackknifed across it.

The second carriage, which bore the brunt of the explosion, tore open across its width, spilling out bodies before it slammed into the first carriage. Three more carriages jackknifed at the tunnel entrance but the two remaining carriages managed to stay facing forward but were tilted over at a precarious angle, revealing their undercarriages. Everything suddenly seemed very quiet.

Golakov continued to film for a few more seconds before he got bored and put his camera away.

Chapter 2

A few minutes earlier.

Jack was just boarding the train when his phone rang. He took out his mobile and saw Randy's face on it. Randy was Jack's *intelligence* officer at ASIO, responsible for keeping Jack informed and up to date with all the data he needed on a mission. He was in his mid-twenties, had middle parted hair, long on top and short on the sides and wore thick rimmed black glasses. Johnny Depp would have been proud of him.

'Hey bud,' said Jack.

'Can you hold up? I got somin to discuss,' said Randy, sounding somewhat out of breath.

'I just got on...'

'Then get off, genius...'

Jack grinned and pushed past some people to get out the doors before they shut. As he did so, the tracker device rubbed against someone else's better quality jacket and the micro barbs found a lot more fiber to adhere to. A piercing whistle shrieked nearby and a second later the doors slid shut behind him. The train began rolling out the station with the tracking device still on board.

He waited on the platform. Randy would be there in a few minutes, he lived near the station in a rented apartment which had great views of the distant harbor and Bondi Beach.

'Did you miss me?' asked Randy as he approached Jack. He was carrying a black shoulder bag over his brown leather jacket. Jack knew that it contained an iPad and a Toshiba notebook which Randy had modified to make it able to run all the current popular operating systems. He claimed that they each had their various advantages and disadvantages. *He probably slept next to it,* thought Jack.

'I missed you like a hole in the head,' said Jack with genuine warmth.

'Ah, ya know that thing that came your way yesterday and, and then it went away again?' asked Randy. He was being intentionally deceptive. He knew better than to discuss case details in public.

'Yeah... big C said it was a computer glitch,' said Jack. Big C was Jack's boss, Benjamin Crowley, a big guy who in his younger days had played Aussie Rules rugby at a national level.

'Well there's something up with that,' said Randy. 'Yesterday, I checked through all the logs and I even back traced and compared them against the data on the remote backup servers and I found no trace of that report.'

Jack waited patiently for Randy to continue.

'But I did find something else out-of-place. The Perl script I wrote compares the local server data with the backup data and spits out any discrepancies. It spat out a comma...' said Randy and looked expectantly at Jack as he waited for the obvious question.

'A comma! What does that prove?' asked Jack.

Randy smiled and said, 'The backup file is a duplicate, an exact copy...'

Jack thought this over for a moment or two and then the penny dropped.

'Someone changed it?' he was both relieved and alarmed at the same time. Yesterday, he had received a report via the internal network about an aboriginal man whose body had been autopsied in Adelaide. The report had been routed to ASIO because the man had died of radiation poisoning. When Jack tried to print the report his computer screen just froze up. He had to shut down and restart his computer and by the time that was done, the report could not be found.

Randy saw the look on Jack's face. 'Yep, I been thinking about it all night. It's impossible for the comma to have shifted in that backup log file other than by human intervention. Someone deleted that report and covered their tracks while you were still looking at it. It continued to be visible to you on your screen until you tried to print it, then the poor little computer got all confused when it tried to print a non-existent file so it crashed.'

Jack thought it over a bit then said, 'Someone in our office...'

'Maybe..., definitely someone with access to our systems, and with our level of security, I doubt it came from outside.'

The public address system interrupted them. '*Ladies and gentleman, CityRail wishes to advise you that all trains on this line have been canceled due to technical difficulties. Buses will be made available but will not be in place for at least one hour.*'

'Let's take my car,' said Jack.

###

Jack pulled his car out of his garage while Randy waited outside. The garage was a tight squeeze.

'I still think you should have gotten this in yellow, it's a much more fun color,' said Randy as he closed the car door. He was referring to Jack's Jeep Wrangler fitted with the Mopar Adventure Pack.

'I agree,' said Jack. 'But I think that the metallic silver blends into the burbs better. If some nut job wants to take me out, I'm not gonna make it easier for them by wearing a bright yellow Jeep around my neck.'

'Nah, you watch too much James Bond. You're just an ASIO field agent. Nobody knows that you exist,' said Randy tauntingly.

'That's precisely how real agents stay alive,' said Jack. 'I don't want to show up on national TV in a bright yellow jeep, wearing a superman costume.'

Jack turned on the car radio as he drove onto Oxford street. The sound of Dire Straights 'Walk of Life' filled the car.

'Wow, that's an old one,' said Randy.

'Yeah I like listening to WSFM, they play all the classics.'

They drove along for a while with Jack tapping the steering wheel to the beat of the music while Randy rocked his head back and forth.

Just as they reached the Sunken Gardens at the Walter Read Reserve, Randy's phone suddenly played a rather dramatic tune, like something from a cheap horror movie.

'Oh crap...' said Randy. 'I programmed the office server to alert me when possible threats are in my vicinity.'

Jack noticed that Randy sounded serious enough, so he dispensed with any jovial taunts. 'How bad is it?'

Randy read the text message which had been sent to his smart-phone. 'Possibility terrorist attack. A bomb just blew up a train near the Sydney Art Gallery.'

Jack was shocked. 'We'd better go check it out then. I'll cut through Kings Cross.'

'No wait a second,' said Randy. 'Traffic might be backed up there. My mapping software gets traffic data from all around the city and I even use live satellite data as part of the algorithm.' He tapped his phone a few times then said, 'Stay on Oxford then take a right onto College Street then head up Art Gallery Road.'

Jack drove up the service road next to the Art Gallery then turned right and parked under some trees. He wanted to be sure they did not block the path of any emergency vehicles. Two police vehicles were already on the scene, having being alerted by witnesses.

Jack and Randy walked across the lawn towards where some people had gathered. Jack estimated that at most, about a half hour must have passed since the event occurred. As he drew near he could make out more and more of the train wreck until he reached the end of the lawn and found himself looking down at the first few carriages which had smashed into the tunnel entrance directly beneath where he was standing. Vehicle traffic had ground to a halt on the expressway and emergency vehicles were struggling to get through. Randy's software had definitely found them a better route.

He looked down at the train below him again. People had obviously died here. *What kind of evil person would do something like this,* thought Jack as he eased himself over the low wall separating the lawn from the drop down to the railway line. He jumped onto the roof of the first carriage and noticed that the overhead power lines had collapsed onto the carriages. He knew more than hoped that the circuit breaker would have tripped as it happened. After all he did not see any arcing between the cable and those items it was touching.

From his vantage point he could see into the gaping hole which tore through the second carriage which was partially crushed against the first carriage. Amongst all the blood he saw a leg which was no longer attached to its owner. No survivors here but on the far end of the carriage things looked more hopeful because there was less severe damage. The only way in was through the hell hole in front of him. Both of the connecting doors of the first two carriages were buried under the collapsed embankments which lead up to the tunnel entrance.

Jack held back for a second and looked over the rest of the scene trying to assess the most effective course of action to take. The first carriage was also partially compressed along its width and three of its four doors were blocked by the second carriage and the embankment wall. The other door was facing the tunnel entrance and was not accessible unless a person could somehow crawl under the carriages. Sending people down the tunnel from the other side was an option but would be difficult and time consuming.

There were other people busying themselves with rescuing survivors from the more accessible rear carriages which in a way made sense given the limited resources on the scene. Fire engines had also arrived via the Cahill Expressway below but the road was blocked with cars which had nowhere to go. Some cars had collided in an effort to avoid what they thought was going to be a train falling on them from the raised tracks and some pieces of concrete and train line had indeed landed on the road below.

Jack heard a faint cry from inside the broken up second carriage, or maybe it came from the first carriage below his feet. He looked up at the gathering crowd above him and yelled 'I'm going in, I think I heard something!' Then he pointed at the carriage beneath him and yelled again 'Can someone find an angle grinder and start cutting through this roof!'

The hell hole looked unconfrontable but Jack steeled himself and lowered his body down through the gaping hole onto the blood soaked tangled metal where the floor of the carriage used to be. Looking towards the rear of the carriage he squinted in the gloom and tried to plot a path. It also smelt funny, and not in a pleasant way.

'Anyone alive in here?' said Jack in a loud voice. Part of him hoped not to hear a reply, he did not want to go in there. He heard a weak reply, and then another. 'Hold on, we gonna get you out as soon as we can,' said Jack. He looked down at the bodies he had to get past and decided it would be prudent to first check their pulses before walking over them and further injuring any that may just be unconscious. Five bodies in he found a pulse, very weak but present. He noticed that this person was loosing blood from a bad wound in the lower thigh area. Jack realized that he had to stop that leak or the person was not going to survive long enough for the medical professionals to get to him. He started looking around for something to use as a tourniquet .

'Here! This should work', said a female voice behind Jack. He spun around and in the dim light he could see a woman ripping a length of wire out of a ceiling light which had popped out of the corner paneling of the carriage. He had not noticed her coming into the carriage. She must have climbed in through the hell hole as well. *Gutsy women,* thought Jack.

'I'll do this one, check the others,' she said without sounding the least bit bossy.

A few minutes earlier, Renae, dressed comfortably in shorts, sneakers and a T-shirt, was standing on the balcony of her apartment with her camera in hand. It was a brand new Panasonic AG-AF101, which she had ordered from a specialist supplier the day before. She needed to familiarize herself with its features so she had brought it outside for some field testing.

It had various modes of exposure which could be tweaked to get the perfect picture for those who knew what they were doing. As a freelance travel and wildlife documentary maker, she certainly had the know how.

In the distance, a train was making its way out of Kings Cross so she zoomed in on it. This was a good opportunity to also test the new shotgun microphone she had bought for an upcoming project. In her headphones, she was pleased to hear the sound of the train with little to none of the traffic sound of the cars on the expressway near her apartment. The microphone had superb directional capabilities. She skillfully kept the train in the viewfinder by zooming in as it neared the tunnel entrance by the Art Gallery when suddenly something exploded and the train derailed and piled up in front of the tunnel entrance.

Renae was stunned, she had caught the whole thing on camera in high-definition video and Dolby digital audio. She went inside, put down the camera and dialed triple zero, Australia's emergency hotline and told them what she had witnessed. Next she decided to go help out at the scene, she had done a lot of training for emergency medical first aid, primarily because her documentary work took her to places where hospitals were a distant luxury. She and her small crew had to know how to take care of themselves in times of trouble.

Her apartment was on the twenty-third floor of a high rise building in Kings Cross and about eight hundred meters from where the train had derailed. She decided it would not be the smartest move to take her car out on roads which were already getting backed up, besides eight hundred meters was a short distance to someone in her excellent physical condition. She took the stairs and started running.

Ten minutes later Renae arrived at the scene. Other people were already there from all around the area or from cars which were passing when the explosion occurred. In the distance she could hear the sound of approaching sirens.

She saw some people trying to smash a carriage window with a rock while another tradesman had brought a crowbar and was trying to force open the carriage doors.

She could see that the front three or four carriages were piled up against the tunnel entrance and would for the most part be inaccessible.

Renae had, earlier in her career, participated in the making of a documentary about train safety and she recalled that the doors would *fail* in the locked position but could be opened from the outside by pushing the EDR button which was concealed beneath a panel near the door. She made her way over to the nearest carriage and quickly located the panel then pushed the big red button. The doors opened. She then carefully negotiated her way over and around more debris and an occasional dead body to the remaining carriages and released the doors via the EDR buttons.

The two carriages nearest the front were impossible to reach and as she stood there wondering how she could get help to those survivors, she noticed a man jump down from the top embankment onto the carriage roof. He hesitated for a moment then began lowering himself into what she assumed was a hole in the roof of the carriage, which was hidden from her view at ground level.

Looking back at the carriages whose doors she had just released, she realized that there was enough help there already. Passengers from within the coach were assisting each other out the doors whilst being aided by people on the ground. She also saw the first of the ambulance emergency responders running up towards some of the injured people. She decided to go help the person who had climbed through the roof of the front carriages.

Jack continued working his way through the carriage, checking pulses. He found another but the light was getting dimmer the further he got away from the hell hole and he could not ascertain the person's injuries.

'I got another but I need light', said Jack in the direction of the woman.

'I got a mini torch on my key ring,' she said while at the same time beginning to move towards him.

He was too focused on what he was doing to even think of social niceties. Asking her name never occurred to him or seemed necessary. She moved right up to where Jack was then using the mini torch she quickly scanned the injured person's body.

'No obvious external injuries here,' she said.

'I agree, lets move on,' said Jack, having made the decision that their time might be better spent on people with field treatable injuries. Apparently his unknown assistant agreed because she was already checking pulses of people on the left of the aisle while Jack continued checking pulses of people to his right.

'Need light here,' said Jack as an arm moved of his own accord when he grabbed its wrist. The torch-light revealed a semi conscious male with an obviously broken lower leg and a lot of cuts and bruises. The leg was bleeding enough to make Jack want to apply another tourniquet to this person as well.

'Hold...' she said as she pressed the mini torch in Jack's hand and magically produced another piece of wire and began applying a tourniquet.

'There were two wires going to that lamp...' she said, sensing Jack's unspoken question.

'Are you a doctor?' asked Jack.

'No, I'm just a regular Renae.'

'You could have fooled me, I'm Jack.'

They both continued working back through the carriage. The injuries became less severe as they progressed. There were still broken bones but none had pierced the skin and there was little that Jack and Renae could do other than help people get as comfortable as they could in the circumstances.

At the back of the carriage Jack suddenly realized that the west-facing sliding door was facing the sliding door of the first carriage and beyond that the open tunnel entrance of the second train line. There was a real danger of another train coming down that tunnel and colliding with these carriages full of injured people. It also provided a means of getting some of these people out and to a hospital, but only if they could open the doors and get some type of transport through the tunnel.

Jack wiped his bloody hands on the back of one of the train seats and took out his mobile phone.

'Randy, do CityRail know that they need to halt all traffic through both tunnels?' asked Jack.

'Yep, I called them myself,' said Randy.

'Good, tell them to back a train down the southernmost tunnel and make sure it has an open rear doorway. If I can get these side doors open then we have a way to get some people out of here by loading them onto that train,' said Jack.

'Good idea master Jack, and I'll make sure they put some medico's on that train and have ambulances waiting at Martin Place to pick them up. I'll also get Cityrail to provide someone who can force those doors if necessary.'

'Alrighty, keep me updated. Bye,' said Jack then he put his phone back in his pocket.

'I know how to open the doors,' said Renae.

'Is there a hidden button here somewhere?' asked Jack while playing the torch over the area next to the door.

'No, it's outside, under a panel,' said Renae. 'They had problems in the past with really stoopid people forcing the doors open while the train was moving. I think the figure was between eight and thirty people a year getting themselves killed like that so they made the decision to have the emergency door release on the outside. The idea being that the train driver and the rear guard would open them.'

'Well that's genius... the train driver is probably dead and the guard guy is most likely injured or in a coma. So now who opens the doors?' asked Jack through clenched teeth.

'I know, and it gets worse!' said Renae, also sounding a bit angered. 'Cityrail ran two simulated train accidents between 2002 and 2004 and the emergency responders did not know how to open the doors either. They were going at it with blunt instruments. Get a bigger hammer and all that.'

'You serious?' asked Jack incredulously. 'I thought they trained them well.'

'I believe they do, on the medical stuff that is. I don't know why the EDR info is not part of that training,' said Renae.

Jack stepped back from the door he was examining and said 'I don't think that the EDR button will help. These doors move to the outside before they slide to the sides.

With these carriages jammed up against each other, there's no space for that outward movement. Besides, this carriage got hit by a bomb. The compressed air lines that powers the doors would definitely have ruptured.'

'So you going with the big hammer approach?' asked Renae.

'Something like that...' said Jack as he pulled out a pistol he had tucked in the small of his back.

'You can't shoot the train!' said Renae with consternation.

'Relax, I'm just gonna try to break the glass in the door.'

Jack gave the glass a tap with the butt of his pistol. Nothing happened. He tried again, much harder and on the third attempt the glass fractured slightly but only at the point of impact.

'Need a bigger gun?' asked Renae.

'No, it's safety glass. Even a big ten pound hammer will have a hard time getting through here,' said Jack.

'That's crazy, why make it impossible for passengers to escape? What if a train derails and lands in a lake or river...' said Renae.

Jack was about to reply when his phone rang. It was Randy.

'Good news bro, they liked your idea. A train will be backing down there in about ten or fifteen minutes. Meanwhile a Cityrail MacGyver and some ambo people are running your way down the tunnel.'

Jack peered through the glass of their carriage doors, through the adjacent carriage doors and could just make out some flashlights bobbing about.

'Yeah, I see them. That's good, nobody has been into the first carriage yet,' said Jack expressing concern.

'I also got a fire-fighter crew up here who are about to lower a ladder down the hole you and that hot blond climbed into. They wanna know if the ladder will be injuring anyone, it's hard to tell from up here,' said Randy.

'It's okay, ... uhm... all the ... errr... those who need help are on the south side, near the doors,' said Jack, trying to be tactful about the situation at the hole. 'Another thing, we've done what we can down here so once the ladder is in place, tell them to let us come up before they send anyone down or we will just be in the way.'

Renae, having heard Jack's conversation, started carefully making her way back to the explosion damaged area.

Jack addressed the injured passengers near him, many of whom were conscious and in pain. 'Medics are coming in so we need to make space for them. There's also a medic team about to gain entry through these glass doors and they will evacuate you onto another train and then to a hospital.'

'Thank you', mumbled a nearby passenger.

When Jack arrived back at the hole the ladder was already in place.

'You first,' said Renae. 'Girls only like attention when they look their best.'

Jack shrugged and started climbing up the ladder. He suspected that Renae's actual reason for being second up the ladder had to do with not wanting him staring up at her butt.

As he emerged out the top of the carriage some cheering and clapping erupted from the crowd on the embankment but faltered noticeably as people saw all the blood that had transferred onto his arms and clothing. It brought home the grim reality of what the circumstances down in the carriage was. A fire-fighters gloved hand helped him onto the embankment where he was immediately questioned by a paramedic team who were about to enter the carriage. He spent the next minute or two briefing them on the situation as best he could and then turned to look for Renae to thank her for her assistance. She was nowhere to be seen.

'She said she was going to get cleaned up.' said a voice behind Jack. He turned around to see Randy grinning at him. 'I think she likes you...' He then pointed towards the Sydney Art Gallery and said 'she went that way, probably to use the nice bathrooms they have in there.'

'Good idea,' said Jack. 'Did she say anything else?' he added hopefully.

'She gave me her number...'

'You dog, you hit on her at a time like this?'

'I tried, but she wasn't interested. The number she gave was for you.'

Jack grinned, his day just got better. He was about to head off to the art gallery when a police detective stopped him with more questions about what he had seen and heard. Jack spent several more minutes answering questions and talking to people on the phone before he caught a break and made his way towards the art gallery. As he did so he noticed a familiar figure break into a comfortable run as she entered the park. She was headed in the direction of Kings Cross and as she exited a patch of trees, she turned, saw him and waved before continuing on. Jack just stood there with one arm half raised in a frozen gesture. He had just realized who she was. In the dim light of the carriage interior he had not recognized her. Renae was the blond surfer he had admired on countless morning runs at Bondi Beach.

Randy stood looking at him and shook his head. 'She said she lives there in that big ass building' he said and pointed at a tall block of apartments some distance away in what appeared to the CBD area of Kings Cross.

Jack and Randy walked the remainder of the distance to the art gallery and as Jack entered the foyer a thoughtful staff member handed him a souvenir T-shirt wrapped in plastic and pointed in the direction of the toilets. Jack looked down at his filthy, blood drenched clothes and said 'Oh wow, I'm probably scaring away your patrons. Got any pants to go with the T-shirt?'

'Sorry, we only have the T-shirts,' said the woman.

Jack decided he would strip off his pants before getting into his car. He would much prefer to keep his seat clean. Once in the toilets he cleaned himself up as best he could, threw his old shirt in the bin and put on the souvenir T-shirt.

Randy looked at Jack's pants and said, 'Tell you what, I can walk to Town Hall from here. Why don't you go back home and get changed. I'll tell Crowley you'll be in later.'

Chapter 3

Jack made a left turn into Kent street and then another into a parking entrance which bore a simple sign saying *462 Kent Street*. He parked in a reserved parking bay whose pole-drop barrier dropped to ground level as his vehicle approached. From there he walked around to the service elevators and pushed the intercom button.

'One coming down,' said Jack and then waited. There was no elevator button for where he was going. The intercom alerted a security guard who then checked a camera feed from inside the elevator. Satisfied that Jack was alone he called the elevator down to the deep basement level which covered the entire area beneath the historic Sydney Town Hall and St Andrews Cathedral. The stable sandstone layer beneath Sydney made it relatively easy and safe to build underground tunnels, parking areas and hidden offices. When an office block was being constructed behind the cathedral, ASIO had bought the lowest floor of the parking area, thirty meters under the office block and then tunneled into the adjacent sandstone to make office space. They also had an elevator going up into the below street level shopping area which runs from Town Hall all the way to Center Point.

When Jack stepped out of the elevator he presented his ID at the security check point and then went into the office to his desk. The desk phone rang and he knew it would be Crowley calling.

'So you got to be a hero this morning,' said Crowley. 'Get yer ass in here to the debrief room.' and then he hung up. Jack wondered why he had bothered to sit down. He knew he would have to get debriefed about the event. He stood up and walked off towards the glass room on the south end.

Jack sat at the long table in the glass room. Randy and a few other agents and intelligence people were also there as well as some strangers whom Jack had not seen before. The strangers did not bother to introduce themselves, they looked like head-offices types, the real deal. Crowley stood in front, trying to put on a good show for the heavy weights. He looked at Jack and said. 'So what's your take on this mornings event?'

Jack knew that Crowley was not interested in the humanitarian aspect. That was only for later when they gave a public pleasing press statement via the Mayor or some other suitable spokesperson. Such press statements were usually very sanitized and often were blatant lies just to keep the public under control and *working* so that the government could get their tax dollars.

Jack glanced around the faces at the table and said, 'From the way the metal was ripped it looked like high-speed explosives were placed either on the track or under the carriage, probably C4 or Semtex. It definitely was not a homemade black powder and fertilizer type bomb.' Jack paused briefly to let them absorb that datum then continued. 'I would say it was placed on the tracks itself because when I looked down the rail line I could see that the tracks were blown clear off the concrete substructure at a point which was about two hundred meters from the tunnel.'

'Probably a contact detonator on the rail,' said another field agent, trying to sound knowledgeable and probably thinking about career advancement.

'Um, no I don't think so,' said Jack cautiously, trying not to rain too hard on the agents parade. 'The blast occurred about a meter and a half past the wheels of the second carriage. A contact trigger would have exploded the bomb under the front wheels of the first carriage.'

'So the second carriage might have been specifically targeted,' said one of the head-office people.

Jack opened his mouth to agree when Crowley cut him off and said. 'It's very unlikely, there are no reserved seats on the trains and the windows are sufficiently tinted so that you can't see clearly enough to identify people from the outside. I can't think of a logical reason to target a specific carriage. It was probably a timer based detonation that just happened to blow when the second carriage went by.'

Head office guy just nodded, so Jack held his tongue. It would be career suicide to argue against Crowley in front of Crowley's seniors. Jack, however, did not buy Crowley's argument. Sydney trains were about 90% on time which left a ten percent chance of a rail bomb completely missing the train and just causing enough public concern to heighten security on all tracks. Only a complete amateur bomber would choose that option. This device was placed on the rails and detonated for a specific target. At this time it was all just speculation. Once a more thorough crime scene investigation was underway they would have more accurate facts to work with.

'Is it possible that a RPG or similar rocket based weapon was used?' asked another head office person.

Crowley remained quiet. He was sticking with his timer theory and a rocket was something which was aimed at a specific target.

'I don't think so,' said Jack. He had thought it safe to speak up because his answer did not go against Crowley's theory. 'The concrete substructure has side walls which are over a meter high which means a rocket would need to be fired at a steep downward angle to make it past the side wall and hit the rails under the carriage. I did not see any location from which you could fire a rocket and get the results we saw.'

Crowley looked suitably pleased and head-office guy seemed satisfied with the answer. He then looked at Randy and said, 'You need to stay on top of the chatter. No one has claimed responsibility yet.'

'Yes sir,' said Randy.

Just then Crowley's PA poked her head in through the door and said, 'I got police chief Bennett on the line. He wants to know what the official statement is going to be.'

Head office guy answered her, 'Tell him to avoid using the word bomb. All we know is that a train derailed and something resembling an explosion was seen. He knows the usual spin to put on it.'

Jack knew that you did not get promoted to police chief level if you did not know how to stroke the press. Telling the public that a bomb went off would have a bad negative impact on train usage until the culprit was caught and everybody felt safe again. If they could not hide the fact of the explosion, they would try to make it seem as if it happened after the derailment, as a consequence of an otherwise benign accident. Or plan B would be to blame the Muslims or some other suitable patsy group if it would get public support for an otherwise touchy subject, like sending Australian troops to Afghanistan. The government had full-time spin doctors working for them to come up with explanations which were suitable for public consumption.

Crowley spoke up again 'Okay people, you know the drill. We need answers, go slap your informants around, buy them pretty dresses... whatever it takes. Get to it.'

###

Golakov was celebrating the success of his mission with two Chinese prostitutes. He had one sitting on his face, laughing away merrily as he fondled her breasts and licked her vagina. The other was bouncing around on his penis. As soon as he neared his climax, he threw aside the face sitter, grabbed the other by the hips and pounded into her until he was done.

'Bring me a beer!' said Golakov, then added 'and my phone.'

Golakov checked his e-mail account and got really angry. The e-mail contained no message but the subject read *breakfast was cold*. It was from their ASIO informant.

He knew it meant that Jack was still alive. This was a problem. If they arranged another public accident for Jack, there was a good chance that another smart investigator might realize that Jack was possibly the target. If they just killed him outright, it would be too obvious. If they *disappeared* him, ASIO would still investigate his disappearance and look into what it was that he was working on before he disappeared. They had to avoid the latter at all costs.

Golakov put aside his phone and sipped his beer. He beckoned at one of the prostitutes and pointed at his penis. She slithered over with a pretense of happiness and began sucking on it.

'Slowly!' he said. He leaned back against the headboard and relaxed. He needed to think and this was the best way to do it.

About ten minutes later the answer came to him in the form of a another e-mail. Once again, it contained no message, but this time the subject read *spotlight on breakfast*. It meant that Jack had somehow gained some public attention. It also meant that it was now near impossible to kill Jack, but it opened another avenue of attack. Jack was now vulnerable to being discredited and Golakov had a brilliant idea of how to do it. He was overcome with a sudden need to share his joy with those less fortunate. He put down his phone and grabbed the prostitutes head.

'If you bite, I'll kill you...' he growled and then forced her head back and forth until he released his load.

After Renae had showered and cleaned herself up, she downloaded the video clip from her camera on to her desktop computer. She then reviewed the video clip on her large 28 inch monitor which allowed her to see every detail of the recording. She had two responsibilities here, one to herself and one to the police. If she just gave it to the police, someone would inevitably leak a copy to the press and she would get nothing out of the deal. Whereas if she negotiated a good price for the clip, the police would still get a copy and she would still retain all the benefits of the deal she had negotiated.

Renae then set about making a low resolution copy of the tape and placed her personal logo across it. It was good enough to prove that she had filmed the event but the poor quality and intrusive logo would prevent anyone else from profiting from it. She then emailed copies to her contacts in the industry with a simple message: *I got full HD, make me your best offer. 12:00 PM deadline*.

A few minutes later the first phone call came in. Renae knew that at least four major Australian channels would be very interested. Some would want exclusive rights but then they would have to cover her losses on sales to the other channels. They also usually wanted the right to on sell the material to other interested parties, big name players like CNN.

Renae was experienced enough to know that she could negotiate herself a slice of the on sell action as well. By 12.00 PM she had finalized an exclusive deal with channel seven. One of their staff had reviewed cell phone media of the event and had recognized Renae as being the person who had entered the second carriage. She negotiated a second deal for exclusive rights to do a studio interview with her about her experiences that morning. They also wanted to interview Jack but she said that she only knew his name and had no contact details.

###

Renae drove her red Mini Cooper up Davey road in Eveleigh then left into the parking lot in front of Channel Seven studios.

'G'day Renae,' said the security guard at the reception desk. He recognized her easily, she was hard to forget. Today she wore a red dress with a scoop neck and flared from the waist down. She had tied her hair back with a red butterfly clip and wore white sandals with half height heels. All carefully chosen to look good on her TV interview.

'Sally's expecting you. Let's get you signed in quickly.'

'Been working out Mike?' asked Renae. Mike looked pleased and a bit embarrassed.

'Ah… er… yes, you know, security and all that,' said Mike. Renae signed the paperwork then stepped through the metal detector, waved cheerfully at Mike then continued on to Sally's Office.

Sally greeted Renae somewhat unhappily. 'You drive a tough bargain.'

'I use expensive equipment,' countered Renae as she placed the DVD in front of Sally.

'Yes I know, we like your work,' said Sally. She watched the few minutes of DVD media. 'Wow, shocking isn't it. Okay, you earned your money.' She passed a three page document to Renae and said 'We'll need your signature on that.'

Renae sat down and went through the document. Satisfied, she then signed and dated the last page. Sally added her signature and said 'Brian is ready for you in studio two A.'

Renae had attended film school and was quite familiar with all the requirements of TV production. First she was whisked off for makeup. Studio lights can make a face look very shiny so men and woman alike had to endure a face powdering to take the edge off. Next, she was fitted with a lapel microphone and a small radio transmitter. Then she and Brian went and sat in the comfy chairs where the interview was going to be held. Technicians moved around and checked equipment in the background. Renae and Brian chatted casually until finally every one was ready.

Brian began by doing an opening introduction and then popped the first question.

'How was it that you came to record the train accident this morning?' Renae explained that she was testing new equipment and just happened to be filming the train when the incident took place.

'What was your reaction?' asked Brian.

'I was shocked,' said Renae, 'I could not believe what I had seen. It took me a few seconds to realize that I was still recording the event. I realized that I should call triple zero so I switched off and ran for the phone.'

'What made you go to the scene of the accident?'

'I've had medical training, you know…, first responder stuff, so I knew I could help. I couldn't just stand there doing nothing while people were dying and I had the skill to do something about it. It was peak morning traffic and the Cahill Expressway was just starting to clog up. Some cars had collided and I knew that the emergency vehicles would have a hard time finding a way through.'

'How did you get through the traffic?' asked Brian.

'I didn't bother with a car, I just ran. It was less than a kilometer away,' said Renae.

Brian was taken aback for a moment. He wasn't used to people talking about a one kilometer run as if it was a trivial matter. He put his attention back on the main theme of the interview and said 'Walk us through what you saw when you got there.'

'I saw three or four carriages on the rail bridge and I saw people at the doors trying to get out. There were also people outside trying to do the same thing. Trying to open the doors I mean. There were other carriages sideways across the tunnel entrance. I knew where the door release mechanism was, so that's what I did first.'

'Hold on,' interrupted Brian, 'how'd you know how to open the doors?'.

'Oh, I did a doco some years ago about train safety,' said Renae. 'It was for internal use by Cityrail employees. I don't know what they actually did with it.'

'Well it's lucky you were there then, hey? Wow, so you opened the doors, then what?' asked Brian.

'Well it wasn't as simple as that, there was debris everywhere and I had to be careful about what I was stepping on and over. I was only wearing sneakers, not safety boots. There was also electrical cable which had fallen down from the overhead feeder. I'm not sure what you call that power thingy on top of the coach. But anyway, they had been knocked down and it was a mess. I thought they might be live but other people had already been touching everywhere and not shocking so I did what I had to.'

'We have some footage sent in by our viewers. Let's cut to that now,' said Brian. The video playback showed the scene much as Renae had described it.

'Is that somebody crawling under the carriage?' asked Brian.

Renae squinted a little as she tried to interpret the poor quality video, then she said 'Oh, I think that's me. I had forgotten about that. I was trying to get to the last carriage but my path was blocked by that carriage that you see me crawling under. The side wall was blocked by some of the electrical cable so the only other way was underneath. Once I had the far side doors open, I just came back through the carriage instead of underneath.'

Brian's mouth moved to say something but no sound came out. He collected his wits and continued, 'So here we see a male figure climbing into the hole in the badly damaged carriage near the front.'

'Yes,' said Renae, 'that's Jack, he was responsible for getting that other rescue train that took away all the injured people from those front carriages. It probably saved about eighty people.'

'How did you meet Jack?' asked Brian.

'I met him right there inside that carriage. We did what we could for the people in there.'

'So wow, he's quite a hero then, you both are. Do we know who he works for?' asked Brian.

'No, it was, er... not a good place for chit-chat. I only got his name,' said Renae tactfully.

'Yes of course, well, Jack, if you are watching, we thank you, and you too Renae. Stellar effort both of you,' said Brian.

'Get out!' yelled Golakov at the two prostitutes. They needed no additional encouragement. He smiled inwardly as he saw them scramble around like scared mice, grabbing high heel shoes and the skimpy clothing they had arrived in. They had insisted on being paid up front and he was done with them for now. 'Out!'

Golakov got dressed then reached for his phone and typed a text message to Todorova. It simply read *30 minutes*. He walked to the window and carefully looked out, checking the windows of other buildings and the streets below. He knew what passed as normal for this area and he saw nothing which gave him any reason for concern. No suspicious panel vans or loitering repair men. He walked quietly up to the door, stood with his back against the side wall and opened the door. Nothing happened, and he had not heard suspicious sounds from within the building or passageway either. He waited another second or two then stepped into the passage, locking the door behind him.

Some time later Golakov met Todorova in the public toilets near the Chinese Gardens in Darling Harbor. This particular public toilet was not busy most of the time and they sat down in adjacent cubicles. Golakov took out a small notepad, wrote a few words in Slavic and passed it under the cubicle wall to Todorova. Once he had read the message, he flushed it down the toilet and left. A few minutes later Golakov flushed his toilet and left as well.

Todorova walked casually along Edgecliff road until he got to Veralma Court then he turned and walked down the side access pathway to the garages at the rear. Jack owned one of the units here and had his own garage. Todorova was well-trained and experienced. He knew that breaking into a unit was risky, neighbors might see or hear the activity or the unit might have an alarm system. These were things which could be circumvented if you had the time to do some proper reconnaissance and preparation but that was not the current situation. Few people bothered to secure their garages unless they had expensive tools or machinery stored in there. In close quarter units like this it would not be the case, or rather, it would be extremely unlikely.

Todorova rounded the back of the building and walked up to the garage as if he owned it. Acting suspiciously would just look suspicious, a rather obvious deduction, but most amateurs would loiter around, check that the coast was clear and generally act in a manner which the real garage owner would never do.

The garage door had no protruding handle, it was of the roll up type. A quick upwards yank on the door confirmed that it was locked. There were two options left. This was either a key-only lock or it may have been retrofitted with a motor-mechanism triggered by a remote garage door opener. If it was the latter, then he would have to abort. Todorova pulled a bunch of keys out of his pocket. They were master keys for the locks of several different manufactures who sold garage doors in Sydney. He inserted the correct key to suit the brand of lock on the door and turned the key, pulling upwards at the same time. The door rolled up a few feet. Todorova bent down, grabbed the bottom of the door and opened it fully.

Once inside, he took out a plastic bag containing a detonator of the same type used at this mornings train explosion. This one had Jack's finger prints on it which their ASIO contact had provided. They had then used the prints to make special latex gloves with the prints glued onto the outer surface and then used that to transfer prints on to the detonator.

Todorova dropped the detonator at the base of the back wall, intending to make it look as if a careless Jack had dropped it there. He was about to leave when he heard footsteps coming down the roadway. Todorova turned his back to the road and took out a tape measure and began measuring the walls as a tradesman might when assessing for a quote on a fit-out. The footsteps passed and continued on. Todorova put away the tape, he was almost done. He closed and locked the door again then took out a small spray can with which he quickly sprayed the lock and the lower part of the door he had touched. The self evaporating liquid in the spray can would dissolve the skin oils and remove his finger prints. To an outsider it would look as if he had just lubricated the lock. Wiping away finger prints with a rag was for amateurs.

###

Golakov was at a self storage unit in Paddington which he had rented under a false name several weeks ago. He had used it for storing some of their mission equipment, small quantities of explosives and so on. He had just removed some items which he wanted to keep but had left enough C4 and other equipment to make it look like a typical field supply point for a rogue agent. He usually wore protective gloves when ever he was here but today he wore the latex gloves with Jack's finger prints attached. He made sure he touched everything.

Chapter 4

It had been a long day at the office. Jack had been busy chasing up leads on the train accident, looking at CSI intel as it came in. He had even been back to the crash site once all the survivors and bodies had been removed. It was one gigantic crime scene and no trains would be allowed to travel on the Bondi line for the next several days, perhaps weeks. Other agents had interviewed witnesses and passengers as far as they could. It was data overwhelm at this point and no definitive answers yet.

Jack pulled into the underground parking garage of Westfield shopping center in Bondi Junction. Randy was with him and they had not spoken much during the journey from Sydney CBD.

'Thanks for the ride bro,' said Randy. 'Wanna come up for a beer?'

'Ah no thanks, I think I'm going to head out to Bondi Beach for a beach run, clear my head a bit. I don't want to see walls and trains for a while.'

'Yeah sure, no worries,' said Randy as he got out the car. Jack also got out and looking over at Randy said 'I'm going to pop into Woolies and get some sausages and eggs. I think I'm gonna cook up a big breakfast tomorrow before I go in.'

Randy laughed and said 'Yeah, Big C can wear you down man.'

'Tell me about it...' said Jack as he walked in the direction of the mall entrance, then looking back said 'Maybe I'll come round later for that beer.' Randy gave a thumbs up and continued walking. He looked tired.

Jack bought two packs of sausages and some eggs. Being single, his grocery buying habits were rather disorganized and spontaneous. He was not sure what he had in his freezer. He remembered buying sausages some time ago but had not kept track of how much was left. It was easier to just buy more and that way he would be sure to have enough for breakfast.

When he arrived back at his Jeep he opened the door and hesitated. It was a summer evening and the temperature was a balmy thirty-one degrees. He would much rather go put his sausages and egg in his refrigerator at home instead of having it in the car for the next few hours at Bondi Beach. It would be a short walk to his apartment and it would also afford him the opportunity to get changed into more beach appropriate clothing. He locked the car door again and started walking.

Jack turned onto EdgeCliff road and continued walking in the direction of his apartment. His thoughts had drifted to Bondi Beach then to Renae. He was going to call her but not tonight, it was too soon and his work situation was too pressing. Most people would plan such things for the weekend but Jack only got to have weekends when it looked like the world was not going to blow itself up for at least two days. He could not see any weekends in his near future. At least ASIO was generous with throwing in some free paid leave at the end of crunch times like the one they were in now.

A red and blue flashing light in the distance caught his attention. As he drew closer he saw several police cars and a large van were completely blocking the road in front of his apartment. Jack stopped walking. The rear doors of the van suddenly opened and eight men in full body armor and automatic rifles piled out and headed towards the apartment building. Four of them split off and ran down the side path next to the building, the other four stationed themselves at the front entrance.

Jack stood transfixed for a moment longer, then turned around and started to walk back the way he had come. He somehow sensed that the activities at his apartment meant trouble for him. Rather than walk in blindly, knowing himself to be innocent of whatever the problem was, his training and instincts were leading him away from the situation. He had to get intel, process the data and asses the situation before taking any course of action. Randy was his intel guy.

'Yo buddy, wassup?' asked Randy when he answered Jack's call.

'I got body armor surrounding my apartment building,' said Jack quietly, still walking casually away from the scene

There was a pause then Randy said, 'I'll call you back in a sec.'

Jack walked on and got as far as the corner when his phone rang.

'You've been burned buddy. Police received a tip-off about explosives from this mornings train wreck being stored at your place and in some storage locker in Paddington.'

'Shit!' said Jack, all tiredness evaporating as adrenalin kicked in. His trained mind started racing through all the possible reasons why this might happen.

Randy interrupted, 'You need to dump your phone mate. They are probably tracing which cell tower it's using as we speak and by now they know you are in the area but won't know your exact location.'

Jack ended the call without saying another word. He turned the corner and was about to toss the phone over the wall next to him when a utility vehicle stopped at the corner. The driver had wanted to turn left but by now it was obvious that something was blocking traffic to his left. He hesitated as he considered alternative routes. Jack took the opportunity to cross the road behind the utility vehicle and as he did so, he casually dropped his mobile phone into some cardboard boxes near the back edge of the vehicle. Some misdirection of police attention was always valuable.

Jack continued walking in the direction of the mall. He would not be able to use his Jeep on the road but it was unlikely that it would have already been detected in the packed parking garage under the mall. He wanted to get his emergency kit out of the trunk before his Jeep became highly obvious in its solitude after the mall closed for the night. He knew that police vehicles were fitted with cameras which extracted license plate information from cars on the road at the rate of thirty a second. His license plates would be on the hot list by now. He could swap number plates with another vehicle in the parking garage but it was a high risk option as well. Parking garages had cameras and security guards watching from a booth hidden out of sight of the general shopping public. Besides, there were probably only about fifty silver Jeeps in Sydney. From now on they would all be regarded with high suspicion.

The parking garage was busy and seemed safe enough. Jack could not see any security types lurking in unusual locations or any of the other typical behavior associated with an upcoming take down. He still had his shopping bag of sausage and egg with him. He felt that it provided a natural cover for his activities in and around a shopping mall. Jack walked up to his Jeep, opened the trunk door and took out a small black bag from within and put it in his shopping back. After locking the trunk door again he headed into the mall and to a public toilet cubicle.

Jack opened the black bag and took out a light brown curly wig. His emergency kit also contained other makeup products, a small mirror, a knife, money, alternative credit cards, false nose and false ID's of various types, half with pictures of him in the brown wig and false nose and half with him appearing as his usual self.

Several minutes later a light brown-haired man wearing Jack's clothes emerged from the cubicle. He walked up to the big mirrors at the wash hand basin and inspected his handiwork. *Looks good,* thought Jack.

He felt a little less tense now, the immediate threat was over. He could easily order beer in a bar full of police and no one would recognize him as a wanted man. Looking down at the shopping bag he considered tossing it but changed his mind. An abandoned shopping bag in a mall toilet could also draw the attention of paranoid rent-a-cops. Jack realized that he was rather hungry and thought he had better go buy some takeaway food while he had the chance. He had no idea what the rest of the night would bring so the smart thing to do would be to use the resources which were there *while* they were there.

He ordered a sandwich from Subway and sat at one of the tables in the food court. A TV screen nearby was showing news highlights and featured the events of the train crash that morning. Jack watched with mild interest, he had seen all the cell phone recordings and interviews and had even questioned many witnesses himself. It was possible that a TV reporter had stumbled onto a witness with something new to say, but very unlikely.

'We are now crossing to an exclusive interview with Renae Thomson who by chance had happened to film the train crash as it happened,' said the TV presenter.

Jack did not immediately connect the dots but almost choked on a mouthful of chicken when he saw Renae sitting in the interview with Brian. It was *his* Renae, the blond surfer who helped him in the carriage that morning. She looked beautiful under the bright lights of the studio. And that red dress, *Oh my God,* thought Jack. He had not seen her like that before, no one got all dolled up to go surfing. Jack watched the interview with his mouth open and a partially chewed bite of chicken sandwich still on his tongue.

'Welcome to Channel Seven again Renae,' said Brian.

'Why thank you Brian, it's always a pleasure.'

'Now Renae, you are a documentary maker. Many of our viewers have watched your documentaries without knowing that it was you making it happen behind the scenes.'

'That's right Brian, Channel Seven has been good to me but of course my biggest local customers would be the documentary feature channels.'

'You mean the government sponsored SBS and ABC?'

'Correct.'

'Yes of course,' said Brian. 'So you managed to capture this mornings train accident as it happened?'

'Yes, I was familiarizing myself with a new camera I had bought for an upcoming project and wanted to test the long-range microphone and some of the other cool features that this camera has. From where I was standing I saw the train coming out of Kings Cross and decided it would make a great test subject.'

'Okay, let's have a look at what you caught on camera, and we want to warn sensitive viewers that the following media contains very graphic material,' said Brian.

Jack watched the train accident as Renae had filmed it. He did not know about the existence of the tape until now. Having gone public with it, Channel Seven would be obliged to hand a copy to the police who would in turn pass a copy on to ASIO.

Jack subconsciously began chewing on his mouthful of sandwich again. He watched the rest of the interview and marveled at Renae's tact and consideration regarding the events that morning. She was quite the professional.

When the interview had run its course Jack's thoughts returned to the earlier film clip.

He had to get a good look at the recording she had made. It may contain clues about why someone had framed him.

###

Renae was on her way to meet some friends for drinks at a popular pub in Bondi. Her interview had gone well and she had made a nice sum of money. Some people might consider it callous to profit from events like this mornings but the reality was that there were always real expenses involved. Fire-fighters and ambulance workers all drew a salary. The Cityrail people who had to clean up the mess would all do so on a salary. News channels would cover the story and earn advertising dollars from the viewers they attracted. In her earlier days as a documentary maker she had agonized over this ethical problem but as time went by she realized that no matter what happened, the world would keep on turning and you would need to pay the toll. Making documentaries was an expensive business and she had to cover her costs regardless of how many people had died.

She had changed back into shorts and a T-shirt. The red dress she wore earlier was very flattering to her figure and it got her a lot of positive attention but there was a time and place for everything. She was very comfortable in her skin and did not need constant attention from other people to feel good about her self. Tonight was about relaxing with friends and enjoying *their* company. It was not about seeing how many heads she could turn, like some teenager who just recently discovered what her breasts could do for her.

The road to Bondi Beach went past the shopping mall at Bondi Junction and just as Renae saw the big red Westfields sign she remembered that she needed blank DVD's. She had used her last three that afternoon when she made copies of the train clip. Aldi were selling them in packs of fifty at a very low price. She also wanted to grab a salad wrap from Mac's. She preferred cooking her own dinner but being out and about meant having to compromise. Renae turned her car into the parking garage, found a convenient parking near the entrance then went and bought two packs of DVD's before heading off to the food court.

Jack was sipping at what was left of the strawberry and pineapple juice he had bought. He had a lot on his mind. Today had been one of those days where you could not see the forest for the trees. All the concentration on the small details of the train bomb had distracted him from the bigger picture of what the target was... until now. He had very nearly been a victim of the train bomb himself, had it not been for Randy's phone call... Jack felt the fog clear out of his head as the full realization came forward. The bomb damage on that second carriage had occurred at the exact spot where he had been when Randy's phone call lured him off the train... and now he was being framed...

Before Jack could make any further connections, someone walked past him and somehow his attention shifted. Was it a familiar perfume? He casually turned his head and saw with amazement that it was Renae, back in casual clothes and with her hair down. She sat down at a table by herself and began sorting through her food purchase.

Jacks mind was racing. He needed to see the film she had shot. Could he trust her? Would she trust him, after all he was now a fugitive? But she would not know that yet. News of him being the *alleged* bomber had not yet been picked up by the media. The police were probably still tossing his apartment at that very moment. She had not recognized him and he would have to explain the disguise. What if she reacted badly? He did not need that kind of attention, especially in a busy food court five minutes away from a police man hunt... looking for *him*. Perhaps it would be best to follow her to her car and then try to explain himself.

Jack kept an eye on Renae and when she got up to leave, he did the same and then followed at a discreet distance, still carrying his shopping bag.

###

Renae had just unlocked her car door when someone called out to her.

'Renae, wait a sec.'

She turned and saw an athletically built guy with light brown hair. He was somehow familiar to her but she could not recall where exactly she knew him from. He seemed friendly enough so she decided to play it out.

'Yes…'

'I'm glad I caught you, we need to talk.'

'Okay…' said Renae still frantically scanning through her memory to try to find an identity for this person who obviously knew her.

Jack could see that she was struggling a bit. He briefly considered using his ASIO alias with the light-haired version of himself but then thought against it. He needed her to invite him into her car and take him to her apartment. She was clearly not going to do that even if he identified himself as *the good guy*. Besides she would be really pissed at him once she discovered he had tricked her in this way. It was best just to be honest with her and take his chances.

Jack came closer and lowered his voice. 'We met this morning. You told me not to shoot the train.' He waited and watched as realization slowly dawned on her.

'But...' she wrinkled her face and peered at his nose intently, then met his gaze again. 'You're wearing a fake nose and a wig...'

'Yes, I'm working undercover, uhm ... look, it's a long story and I can't discuss it out here.'

Renae considered this latest information. She had earlier assumed he was perhaps some type of police detective. No ordinary person would do what he did that morning and he clearly had connections. Just one phone call from him and Cityrail had kicked a bunch of passengers out of another train so that they could use it as a makeshift ambulance to rescue people via the tunnel. It seemed plausible that he would be here now with questions. But in a disguise?

'Alright, how can I help?' said Renae.

'It's really important that I take a look at that film you shot this morning.'

'I already gave a copy to the police about two hours ago.'

'Our department won't get a copy of that DVD until tomorrow and I can't wait till then.'

'Our department?' asked Renae.

Damn, this woman was no pushover, thought Jack. He took his emergency kit out of his shopping bag and showed her the ASIO ID card with his real picture on it. Dark hair and a curious Asian - European looking face.

'ASIO?' said Renae quietly, sensing that Jack did not want this information blurted out.

'Yes, Australian Security Intelligence Organization,' said Jack patiently. He knew that, unlike the American FBI, ASIO kept a low profile and were hardly ever even mentioned on national television. Most of the Australian public would stare at you blankly at the mention of ASIO.

'You're a bloody government spy?' she whispered.

'Investigative field agent,' said Jack.

Neither of them spoke for what seemed like a very long moment. Finally Renae broke the silence and said. 'Well, you had better get in then.'

Jack stood on the balcony at Renae's apartment and looked out in the direction of the train crash site. The view was distant but unobstructed. He studied it for a while longer, then turned and walked back inside.

'Nice view you have here,' he said to Renae as she waited for her computer to boot up.

'Yes, it's lovely. It gets even better with a glass of red wine.'

'Wow,' said Jack. 'You have really invested in some fancy computer equipment. Why do you need three big monitors?'

'I do a lot of video editing from here. Why pay someone else when I can do it? The editing software I use allows me to split various sections of the software onto different screens which means I can see everything I need at a glance. It actually saves a lot of production time.'

'So you are a bit of a computer nerd then?' asked Jack.

'Nerd! I'm not the one wearing a wig and a fake nose,' said Renae with a big smile.

'Yes, I suppose it may look that way. I know it may seem a bit paranoid but I have reason to believe that this mornings train bomb was intended for me,' said Jack as he walked towards the window. 'I will need to close these blinds before I can take off this stuff. My presence here might be putting you in danger as well.'

Renae nodded an acknowledgment and Jack proceeded to close the blinds on the large windows. The light was beginning to fade outside anyway so it would not seem out-of-place to anyone who might be watching. Jack took off the wig and the latex nose and said 'Tadaah...'

Renae switched on some overhead ceiling lights then, looking at Jack, she said 'That's much better, I'm not used to all this cloak and dagger stuff.' She was about to sit down again then said 'Actually, I think I need some coffee first. I'm starting to think that this might be a long night. You want?'

'Sure, milk and one sugar. Which way is your bathroom? I want to wash off this face makeup I used to blend that latex nose with my skin.'

Renae pointed casually at an open door which was visible in the short passageway then added a good-humored taunt, 'Makeup Jack? Is there something else I should know about you?'

'Yes... there's sausage and egg in that shopping bag I brought. You may as well take it. I won't have a chance to use it for a while,' replied Jack, intentionally not taking her bait.

They met back in front of Renae's editing desk and sat down in two high back wheeled chairs.

Renae took a sip of coffee and said, 'Before we get into watching this video, why don't you fill me in about why you think you were the target. I mean... why would someone kill all those people just to get one person. It makes no sense.'

'That's exactly the reason someone might do that if they wanted to hide the fact that they were targeting one person. I know it seems unbelievable but we have come across this type of thing before. The fact that it does not seem likely or does not make sense is what they depend on to keep it hidden.'

Renae looked at Jack directly and said, 'Okay, I get that, but why you. What did you do to get you deaded.'

Jack realized that Renae was using cute euphemisms to keep the conversation from getting too serious. He was about to explain but hesitated. If they who had tried to kill him knew that she also had knowledge of what was going on then they might want to kill her too. But then again they had switched tactics once the media had painted him a hero. Renae was much more of a publicly known figure and that would probably keep her safe. He decided to proceed cautiously.

'Yesterday, I came across a report of a male Aboriginal who had died of radiation poisoning at an Adelaide hospital. That report then vanished off our systems. Randy found evidence that an insider may have deliberately deleted the file and covered their tracks. This morning I was on that train that derailed but I got off at the last second. The bomb that destroyed that carriage was exploded at the exact spot I was standing before I got off. I did not connect the events until about an hour ago when I got set up as the fall guy for that train bomb.'

'What do you mean you got set up?' asked Renae.

'The police received a tip-off that there was some type of evidence implicating me. They were raiding my apartment in Bondi Junction just a few minutes before I met you in the parking garage at Westfields. It will probably be all over the news in a while.'

Renae looked confused. She ran her hand through her hair and said, 'I still don't get it. By now the public are all aware of what you did to save those people this morning. It would not make any sense to present you as the person who planted the bomb. I can't see the public falling for that.'

'Ah,' said Jack knowingly. 'You aren't familiar with government agency tactics. Many of them play dirty tricks. If they need to eliminate a problem or threat, they have two broad options. Kill or discredit. If a person is too much of a public figure then they usually discredit them... you know... prostitutes, racism, homophobia, drugs, bla bla bla. There are endless possibilities but if the person is clean, then they have to manufacture a lie to discredit them. In my case I'll bet they will be making me look like one of those people who create a problem so that they can go in and be the hero. There have been cases of firemen lighting fires just so that they can get attention when they go save the day. I think there is some technical term for it but I'm not up to date on psycho babble.'

Renae looked astonished. ' I'd hate to do your job. Always watching your back. Not knowing if someone is trying to play you or if they are being genuine.'

Jack looked at her and hesitated long enough to get her attention, then said, 'Actually you've left your self wide open for a similar ... uhm, opportunity... to be discredited.'

'What do you mean?' asked Renae defensively.

'Think about it. You just happened to be in the right place and time to film the bomb exploding. Then you swoop in and become a hero saving people. Then you appear in a TV interview about the event which features the video you recorded of the train bomb. And I'll bet you got paid handsomely for that video. Oh, and I almost forgot. You're a frigging train expert... I mean those EDR buttons. No one else knew how to open those carriage doors...'

Renae looked livid, she pointed a finger at Jack and said, 'Listen bozo, I am completely within my rights to charge for my services...'

Jack cut her off. 'Renae, chill. I'm not accusing you of anything. I'm letting you know how easy it is to set someone up. An agent could sneak in here and leave just a trace of explosive somewhere. Perhaps a few crumbs of C4 in the trunk of your car. Take that along with the scene I just painted and you would look as guilty as Clinton getting a blow job from what's her name in the blue dress.'

Renae, still angry, thought it over for a few moments. 'Okay, I get it. I suppose now that they framed you it becomes even easier to frame me. I mean, we both came out looking like heroes today. It's just a short leap from there to assume that we were in it together.'

Jack was impressed. He smiled and nodded his head. 'Yes… that's why I need your help. I'm hoping that somewhere on that video will be a clue about who was behind this. Whoever they are, they could easily set you up as well because doing that really makes me look even guiltier. I'm surprised they did not go that route actually. My guess is they were pressed for time.'

Renae was now beginning to see the gravity of the situation. 'It's a good thing they don't have my physical address then,' she said smiling.

'What do you mean?'

'I use a post box for all mail correspondence and that box is registered to my uncle's business. This apartment also belongs to my uncle. He's into real estate and has many apartments here in Sydney and on the Gold Coast. I have not given this address to anyone and the bills, you know, water… gas and so on all get paid from his business account.'

'Nice uncle, what's in it for him?'

'He's a shareholder in my documentary business. Keeping my production costs down means more profit for him. Trust me, he's not loosing on the deal.'

Jack pondered this briefly then said, 'What about your Internet? They can trace the I.P. address... I think... I wish I could call Randy. He's the real computer boffin who knows all those details.'

'Well I'm not as clued up as Randy,' said Renae, 'but I'm using 4G mobile Internet and it's registered to my uncles business as well. I'm pretty sure it can only be traced to a cell tower.'

'That's true. Look, perhaps we are being too paranoid but I think from now on you had better be careful about being followed and so on. Watch where you park your car. You don't want to make it easier for them if they decide to set you up as well.'

'Alright,' said Renae, then pulling at her hair she added, 'This is so frustrating... You do realize that technically I'm harboring a criminal right now.'

'I'll leave just as soon as we've had a good look at that video,' said Jack, being a gentleman. He was rather hoping to spend the night here instead of at a hotel.

'Don't be silly,' said Renae. 'I think our paths have crossed for a reason. You can use the couch in the lounge.' Their eyes met briefly.

'Well okay then,' said Jack feeling a bit awkward. 'Fire up that video will you.'

Jack and Renae spent the next several minutes watching and re-watching the video in minute detail until eventually Jack noticed something.

'Look there… right at the edge of the screen. There's a guy with a video camera pointed in the direction of the train crash… then … you see… he just walks away real slow and casual.'

'You're right,' said Renae. 'That's not normal behavior by a long shot. You would think he would make a phone call or get help or go try to help.'

'Can you blow it up a bit?' asked Jack.

'I can but it's going to be pixelated or blocky in layman terms. It's not like on TV where they bullshit the public with fantastic zoom in pictures obtained from low resolution security cameras. The best you can get is this …' said Renae as she presented a large version of the man with the camera.

'Well we certainly can't identify him from that…' said Jack, looking at the screen, 'but we can tell that he is a well-built guy with a rounded face and dark hair. Looks like one of those Scottish guys who toss the lamp pole for kicks.'

'It's called a caber, I think...' said Renae.

'What?'

'Your lamp pole, Jack...'

'Oh...okay, not important in the grand scheme of things. He looks foreign to me, not typical Australian. Can you save that blow up to a USB drive, I want to get it to Randy in the morning.'

'I could just email it to him...' said Renae.

'No, they will be watching him, waiting for me to make contact. An email could be traced back to you and I don't want anyone to make that connection.'

Renae gave a worried look at Jack and asked, 'Then how are you going to get this to him?'

'I know where he goes for coffee in the morning. I'll put on my surfer disguise and slip it to him.'

Jack thought a bit more and added, 'I'll also need to set up a secure means of communication between the three of us and get the details to him as well.'

'You make it sound like you are going somewhere,' said Renae.

Jack looked Renae in the eye and said, 'I have to… tomorrow. The only two leads I have, are this guy with the camera and that radiation problem in Adelaide. Somehow they must be related to the train crash and me being framed for it. I'll let Randy do what he can with that blow-up image and I will have to go to Adelaide and see what I can dig up there.'

That night, Jack had set up a secure chat room and message board which required a person to log in with a user name and password. All communications to and from that server were automatically encrypted and hidden from any prying eyes. Still, to be sure, he had instructed Renae to be cryptic and not to use any actual names and places unless it was absolutely necessary. He had then hand written the web address and log in details on a piece of paper for Randy.

Renae had also given Jack an old Android smart-phone she was no longer using. It was linked to her uncle's account and was therefore unlikely to be traced back to Jack or Renae. It would allow him to get access to the secure server and leave messages. He was not going to use it to directly contact Randy or Renae.

This morning Renae had made breakfast using Jack's sausage and eggs which he had bought the previous night. She had added some bacon and fried up some tomato and onion to go with it.

Jack was still tasting it as he walked along Park street which cut through Hyde Park. He was on foot for various reasons, mostly because Renae's apartment was only 1.5 kilometers from Town Hall on George street and the coffee shop where Randy like to grab a morning cup of coffee before going into the office. Renae had headed out to Bondi Beach for her usual morning run. Jack had explained that it was necessary for her to continue doing what she normally did. Any sudden changes in behavior would attract attention if they were observing her.

Jack did all the usual tricks to make sure he was not being followed. He used shop windows as mirrors for observing the roads and pavement behind him. Following a person on foot was different from following in a car. Most importantly, you could no longer hide inside a car. If you wanted to follow you had to get out and be visible on the pavement. Most people out and about this early were either heading to work, walking purposefully, or they were exercising, doing a brisk walk or a jog. Jack was intentionally changing his pace from a slow saunter to a brisk walk, only stopping to check shop windows. Anyone following would have to be brilliant to not get tripped up and look out-of-place.

By the time Jack got to George street he was satisfied that nobody was following him and therefore it was also unlikely that any agents were watching Renae's apartment, or if they were, they had failed to make the connection with him, which was good. Having crossed *being followed* off his list of worries, he now focused on looking for people watching the coffee shop that Randy frequented. It was much more probable that they might be watching Randy to see if he contacted him.

Jack had figured it was too risky to go and sit down next to Randy and ask the time or act like a tourist and ask directions. Despite his disguise, it was still suspicious activity. If he, Jack, had the job of watching someone to intercept a contact, he would regard all such exchanges as suspicious and put a tail on any such people. ASIO agents were purely investigators however and would need to work with undercover federal police if they wanted to do an actual arrest or detainment for questioning. Jack was now a high value fugitive so there were sure to be undercover police just waiting to pounce. He would have to be very careful and find a safe way to get his message to Randy.

Randy had not slept well at all. Police had raided a house where they thought Jack was hiding out. The plumber who lived there had been apprehended and taken in for questioning until the early hours of the morning when police finally found Jack's mobile phone at the bottom of a box on the back of his utility vehicle in his garage. The last call made from the phone was to Randy and they had sent federal agents to search Randy's apartment, at 1:00 AM in the morning. Randy had figured that they had not had time to record Jack's phone calls so he lied and said that Jack had phoned to tell him he might be coming around for a beer later but that Jack had never shown up. It was 3:00AM before they left and he was really tired.

He was also a bit relieved. It seemed as if he was in the clear for now. It was Jack who had approached Crowley and made a fuss about the report which had gone missing. Randy's involvement had not been mentioned and it seemed that whoever had set up Jack was unaware that Randy had uncovered some clues that the report had been deliberately deleted by someone. He knew he was going to be watched though. They had determined that he and Jack were occasional drinking buddies and sometimes did some car pooling to the office. But that was all they had and they would keep a close eye on him to see if any new leads could be extracted from that connection.

Randy sat in his usual seat at Gloria Jeans Coffee that morning. He knew that Jack would eventually find a way to make contact. A cute waitress brought his coffee to him and he eyed her somewhat expectantly. Perhaps Jack had paid her to somehow put a message in the bottom of his coffee, or under the mug. Perhaps she was wearing something which was meant as a clue.

'Everything alright sir?' she said, thinking she had missed part of his order.

'You tell me,' said Randy carefully.

'Excuse me?' she said looking confused.

'Oh, I meant… would er could I get one of those pear and raspberry slices?' then he dug out a five dollar note from his pocket and said, 'Keep the change.'

'No problem sir.'

Randy used his peripheral vision to observe the area as best he could. A man was standing looking in a shop window some distance to his right. The shop sold woman's clothing and the man seemed way to interested judging by the amount of time he had loitered there. It was not Jack, the build was different and besides, Jack was much smarter than that. The man was either unusually liberated or he was an undercover cop doing a bad job of covering that avenue of escape.

Some distance to his left he saw two woman engaged in conversation, but somehow they did not look relaxed enough. It was one of those things that he could not directly point out as being wrong but it just did not seem quite right either. They might also be federal police waiting for Jack to make contact.

'Here you go sir, will there be anything else?' said the waitress, eying him a bit suspiciously.

'How about your phone number?' said Randy. He knew it was lame but he was nervous. Jack was the expert at this field stuff, not him. Anyway, she was cute.

'Have a nice day sir,' she said and left, looking pleased with herself.

Randy ate his pear and raspberry slice. It was nice but had no hidden messages in it. He drank his coffee carefully, not wanting to choke on whatever Jack may have left at the bottom of his cup. He got to the end of it and it had no message in it, nor under it. It even tasted normal.

Damn, he thought. Where was Jack? Randy sat around for a bit longer, giving Jack as much opportunity to make contact as possible but eventually Randy gave up and decided he had better go to the office and endure another day of Crowley-ism.

Jack was having egg on toast at Milly's, a small café on the route from Gloria Jeans to *the office*. He was not hungry but had bought the food because he needed an excuse to sit there and wait for Randy to walk past.

A few minutes earlier, he had walked right past Gloria Jeans and seen Randy chatting to a waitress. He had also seen at least four undercover agents or police doing their best to be inconspicuous. One of them was cleaning a patch of floor with a mop and pail but did not seem like he had anything else to clean because he kept going over the same area. It was a standard setup with agents posted at the available exit points and one or two nearby the target, who would attempt the initial intercept.

After what seemed like an unusually long time, Jack spotted Randy's hair mop and thick rimmed glasses among the morning crowd of people headed his way. He got up and started heading in Randy's direction. People were weaving in and around each other and there were the usual idiots who saw a friend and had stopped right there to chat, causing a blockage that other people now had to navigate around. Jack adjusted his pace to arrive at one of these blockages at the same time as Randy. He timed it to perfection and stepped around the blockage straight into Randy then quickly stepped around him and continued walking on, past Gloria Jeans, noticing that the mop and pail had been abandoned.

As Randy headed towards Town Hall he felt an unusual pressure in his shirt pocket. He instinctively brought his hand to his chest to feel what was in his pocket and almost stopped walking when he felt the package there. *How the hell had Jack done that,* thought Randy. His mind raced. He figured it was a thumb drive based on its size and it was wrapped in paper, possibly a note from Jack.

Why would Jack bother with a note, he could have just left a text file on the thumb-drive as well.

Still walking, Randy stuck his hand in his shirt pocket. The note was just loosely wrapped around the thumb-drive so he pulled it out. Scrawled in Jack's handwriting it read:

Thumb-drive has blow-up image from far right of Renae's video.

secure comms at 252.36.231.87:2067

user = floppyhair

pass = changemefast

Now eat this note

He had no idea what the reference to Renae's video meant. He assumed it would become clear soon enough, so he memorized the other details then crumpled the small piece of paper and put it in his mouth. He had not eaten paper since he was a kid. This was just a small piece but still not a pleasant experience. He had to get it quite wet and soggy before it would slide down his throat.

He left the thumb-drive in his pocket. ASIO's computer network was split into two sections. There was a general office network for low risk Internet research where staff could use the Internet and do pretty much what the general public could do. The only difference was that these computers had special software to aid with locating and accessing data on the external network.

The secure network was on a completely different system with no link to the general network or the Internet. Nobody, not even the best Chinese or Russian hackers could hack that system simply because there was no physical connection between that network and the outside world.

It even used a different network protocol which meant that the two networks did not even speak the same network language. The computers in this area also had no input other than a keyboard. They were essentially dumb terminals designed to give researchers a one way window into the vast data resources available on the secure networks. These terminals were all kept in a separate area and users had to swipe their access cards to get into that area. The upside of this method was that users did not have to be subjected to constant body searching to catch people stealing data.

You could take a thumb-drive into this area without a problem because there was nowhere to plug it in. You could not steal information unless you photographed it from the computer screen which was nearly impossible due to constant surveillance. The system also kept track of who looked at what data and when. That way, if any data was leaked at some point, it could be traced back to the people who looked at that data.

Getting new data onto the secure network was especially stringent. The person providing the data was logged along with time, date, data type, form of media data was taken from and so on. The data was then scanned for viruses and other malware and no live executable code was ever allowed onto the secure network as a data upload. It had never been breached.

All these thoughts and considerations where thrashing about in Randy's mind when he passed through ASIO security access and entered the general area. Randy was not going to risk loading the image Jack had provided, onto the secure network to try an identify it. It would provide a too obvious link back to him. He decided he was going to dump the thumb-drive in the basket of incoming data and cell phone movies from the scene of the train accident. The agent responsible for uploading all that data to the secure network would assume it came from a public source and it would be filed that way on the server and be traceable only back to that agent. They would know to run facial recognition because it was standard practice and Randy just had to keep an eye out for the results.

Chapter 5

Adelaide airport was no busier than usual. Jack had been through there many times before but this was the first time he used his light-haired alias. Jack's looks were a blend of Western and Asian which gave him the very useful ability to blend into both worlds and use either Western or Asian aliases depending on which best suited the occasion. He had bought his airplane ticket under the name of Chikamasa Hiro, a name which meant good and wise. It was a local flight so there was no scrutiny from customs but Jack thought that an Asian name would throw off any agents who might be scanning passenger names for known aliases which Jack had used on official ASIO missions.

Jack had taken only a small bag of carry on luggage, a few items he had bought just before leaving Sydney that morning. He looked at his one way ticket as he was about to toss it into a nearby bin. The name reminded him of the first eight years of his life spent in Japan. His farther, Mick, an Australian, had worked in Japan when he met his mother, Akiko, an artist and singer. They had fallen in love, had married and soon afterward she had given birth to twins, a boy and a girl. Jack's farther, who was always in a good mood, had named them Jack and Jill, from the nursery rhyme. When Jack was eight, the family had moved back to Australia. Jill now lived in Melbourne and was also making headway in the music industry. Mick and Akiko ran a theater production company and had brought many great productions to 'The Lyric Theater' at Star City as well as the Opera House, Sydney's famous landmark.

By now his family would have heard that Jack was wanted for questioning in relation to the train derailment. It would have been tough on them but they would surely know that it could not be true. Jack felt some anger well up. This con job he had become a part of was now affecting people he cared about. He could not contact his family and tell them anything about what was going on. Surely the press would be hounding them for statements and photos. Jack sighed internally and tossed the ticket in the bin. He had not bothered with a return ticket because he had no idea where the investigation would lead him. Besides, no agent worth his salt ever bought a return ticket with a fixed return date. You always had to keep your enemies in the dark about your plans.

He checked the time on his new watch, it was 12:45 PM. Jack had gone to an electronic gizmo shop in Sydney that morning, looking for a Geiger counter or similar device for detecting radiation. He was about to investigate a case of radiation poisoning which meant he was also likely to eventually encounter the source of the radiation and it would kill him too unless he had a way of detecting it.

The electronic shop had various hand-held devices but they were too obtrusive. He did not want something that attracted attention. The shop owner had then produced a Polimaster PM1208, which was an ordinary digital wrist watch by appearance but it contained a tiny internal

Geiger-Muller detector. It was perfect but expensive, costing nearly $800. ASIO would have to reimburse him once he had cleared his name.

This device had a major shortcoming however, the Geiger-Muller tube could only detect gamma rays, it was useless for detecting heavy alpha and beta radiation created from the decay of plutonium and radioactive uranium. The good news was that such substances were often contaminated. Jack had been taught that for plutonium, the best technique was to detect the accompanying contaminant Am-241, which emits a 60-keV gamma ray. Jack's wrist watch detector could therefore give some form of early warning, unless the source material was an extremely pure alpha or beta emitter.

The airport had many car rental agencies and Jack headed over to the Avis booth where he rented a class A vehicle, the cheapest and least likely to attract thieves and other unwanted attention. Then he drove off in the direction of the Royal Adelaide Hospital.

The report Jack had seen did not contain the names of any doctors or staff who had treated or handled the patient which had allegedly died of radiation poisoning. He had made an assumption that if the persons' illness was undetermined it was likely to end up at *The Infectious Diseases Clinical Service* department, so that's where Jack went first, straight to the department administrators office.

Jack presented a fake business card from a real person and said 'Hello Doctor Armstrong. I'm Ambika Yohinda from the Department of Health.'

'Hello Mr Yohinda ,' said the doctor while looking at the business card. 'I see you are an investigator?'

'Yes,' said Jack smiling confidently. 'I realize that you are busy so I'll get directly to the point. We got word that your hospital recently handled a case of radiation poisoning. Naturally we need to follow-up on that and... get to the bottom of the situation to find the source of the radiation and prevent any more harm. Can you tell me anything about that case?'

'Radiation poisoning?' asked the doctor looking dumb founded.

'Yes,' replied Jack and stared at the doctor as if expected nothing less than full coöperation. He knew that as a pretended authority figure, the less he spoke the more the other person would feel the need to tell what they knew and end the uncomfortable conversation.

'I don't know anything about that...' said the Doctor, suddenly feeling guilty about not knowing everything that went on in his department. 'Uhm... hold on let me check with... Doctor Marsh.' After a brief phone conversation he continued, 'I'm sorry, are you sure it was this department?'

'I can't be sure of the department,' said Jack. 'The report I was given stated that an Aboriginal patient was brought in and it was discovered during autopsy that he had died of radiation poisoning. Now... I checked with hospital admin and they said that it was most likely that the patient would have been treated as a possible infectious disease patient until a more accurate diagnoses could be made.'

'Yes, we do handle some unknowns but I assure you that we have not had anyone diagnosed with radiation poisoning, not in the three years I have been here.'

Jack considered alternative options and asked 'What if he came in with a predetermined diagnoses of radiation poisoning... where would they put him?'

'In general ICU, he would be very ill and in need of intensive care... but I would have heard about it if it had happened that way'

Jack considered this information. It was quite plausible that Doctor Armstrong would have heard about a case of radiation poisoning, even if another department handled it. Doctors tended to chat amongst each other about those things they found interesting and a case of radiation poisoning was rare enough to make it to the interesting list. Another idea occurred to him. The patient may have been deceased or died en-route to the hospital. He looked at the doctor and asked in a more polite manner, 'What if he was DOA?'

The doctor sensed that he was probably off the hook for somehow being blamed for mismanagement of the matter and he relaxed noticeably. Looking more confident he replied, 'Oh, in that case he would have gone straight to the morgue. A state forensic pathologist would have taken it from there.' Doctor Armstrong was already opening the door for Jack to leave, eager to be rid of him.

Jack walked along a wide passageway in the basement of the Royal Adelaide Hospital. He had decided to check in with the hospital morgue first before going to the city morgue where the autopsy would have been carried out. He needed to know if they had received the body of the Aboriginal man and if so, where the body had come from. The city morgue may also have that information but Jack's experience had taught him that speaking to many witnesses was usually better than speaking to one. You could learn many things by watching a person's emotional response to a question or situation and a tiny piece of information might become a vital clue at a later date. Anyhow, he was already in the hospital, he may as well find out what their morgue knew about the body in question.

The air down in the basement was less pleasant than up in the hospital. It got worse when he entered the morgue proper. It was the kind of smell that had no other equal. Only a morgue smelt like this and Jack instinctively took small shallow breaths. It was not exactly a stink or a strong pungent smell but it was a rather subtle cheesy smell. On top of that it seemed as if his own body instinctively knew that death was near and it wanted to flee the area with or without his permission. But he took charge and pressed forward past some empty steel autopsy tables to an office area where he could see a man seated at a desk. He knocked briefly on the glass door and walked in without waiting for an invitation. He had decided to go with pretending to be a pushy Federal Police detective and had put a shiny gold and red badge on his belt.

'Hello mate! I'm detective Brown. Sorry to barge in but we got an urgent case and I need some quick info,' said Jack, then pointing a finger at the ceiling he added, ' They told me I would find you here.'

The morgue attendant was still in overwhelm but his social conditioning kicked in and he found himself saying, 'Oh… sure… how can I help?'

'That Aboriginal DOA who came in here recently… remember that?', said Jack leaning on the desk and looking down at the morgue attendant who was still sitting in his chair.

'Uhm… yeah… but city morgue collected him. We don't have him,' he said hopefully.

'I know that… what I don't know is how he got here or where he came from.'

'Oh… he… er… came from… SA ambulance delivered the body, they said it was DOA to them via flying doctors.'

'What do you mean flying doctors?' asked Jack.

'RFD… they brought the guy in from the outback. He died on the plane.'

'Alright… gotcha, thanks,' said Jack and then left as if he had to be somewhere else urgently. Actually he just wanted to get outside into fresh air.

###

While driving to the city morgue, Jack had gone over all the possibilities presented by the data he had uncovered so far. An Aboriginal man from the outback which was a vast area covering about 90% of Australia. Anywhere remote was considered *outback* and he would have to narrow that down to a specific place. There were uranium mines out there in the outback but uranium in its natural state was not radioactive or nobody would be able to mine it. Uranium had to be made unstable and radioactive and further refined into plutonium and that was a complicated and expensive process. It was therefore not possible that a miner had somehow tripped and stumbled onto a seam of uranium which could kill him by radiation poisoning. Perhaps he worked in a uranium enrichment plant and had somehow been exposed but then surely news of that would have gone via regular channels. Uranium enrichment facilities had strict codes of conducts and safety rules to follow.

The autopsy would have uncovered more information about what type of radiation had killed the man. It was either accidental exposure or less likely, intentional use of radioactive material as poison by ingestion.

Jack showed his fake federal police ID at the gate and parked at the back of the city morgue building. As he entered the interior offices he was pleasantly surprised to find it filled with fresh clean smelling air. Perhaps the Royal Adelaide Hospital budget was allocated more to the living than the dead with morgue fresh air being a low, if any, priority. Here at the city morgue thing were clearly different and much better funded. Jack inquired at the nearest desk as to who the senior person was and was directed to find someone called Julie in another glass enclosed office down the corridor. Here and there he saw staff going in and out of doors to his right. He assumed that was where the more grisly details were attended to.

As Jack neared the office he had been directed to, a blond mature woman walked out and upon seeing the badge on Jack's belt she stopped and said 'G'Day detective, were you looking for me?' She was obviously used to dealing with police.

'Yes,' said Jack. 'I'm detective Brown. I just need to see the autopsy report of a case you guys handled recently.'

'Why don't you just do it via the network?' asked Julie, seeming a bit confused. Autopsy reports would have been available to federal police via their internal network.

'Ah...' said Jack. 'That would have been easier except we don't have a name or a case number.'

'How's that happen?' asked Julie. 'We catalog everything as we do it.'

'Possibly a computer problem,' said Jack. 'All I know is that an Aboriginal man was brought in here by RFD from the outback. He was DOA and you guys did the autopsy. I need cause of death.'

Julie brought her hand up to the side of her head and slowly ran her hand through her hair as if pulling out memories from within. After a few moments she said, 'Yes I remember hearing something like that. Doctor Palmer would have done the autopsy...' Her voice trailed off a bit and Jack could see there was a problem.

'Can I speak to Doctor Palmer then?' asked Jack.

'I'm afraid not,' said Julie quietly, looking a bit stressed. 'He was killed in a house fire last night.'

'I'm so sorry to hear that,' said Jack. He was shocked. He instinctively scratched the side of his head as he considered the problem. Was it possible that Doctor Palmer was murdered to hide what he was working on. Jack still needed to see the autopsy report, so he pressed on, 'Would you be able to get access to that autopsy report for me?'

'Yes,' she said, and turned back in the direction of her office. Jack followed her in and waited in front of her desk while she worked at her computer. After a few seconds she said, 'I'll just have to look through what he was working on last week. I'm not sure, but if I recall correctly, that case came in early in the week.' Julie stared intently at the screen, occasionally tapping on the keyboard as she read through the cases which Doctor Palmer had worked on. After a while she said, 'That's odd, there are no cases filed for Tuesday.'

'Was he in that day?' asked Jack.

'Yes, he never missed a day. I don't see any other Aboriginal cases in that week,' said Julie. She continued looking at the screen for a while longer, then finally, she sat up straight and looked at Jack perplexed, 'It's not there.'

Jack shifted his gaze to the corner of the room while he considered options. After a few moments he asked, 'Do you have any other records on that case?'

'Such as?'

'I need to know his name, and where he came from.'

Julie thought for a moment, lifting her eyes to the ceiling as she did so, then she began typing on the keyboard again. Jack noticed that she was beginning to get frustrated. He waited patiently, already knowing what to expect. After what seemed like a long time, she looked at Jack suspiciously and said, 'There's nothing there, it's like it never happened.'

'Our computer glitch must have affected your systems as well,' said Jack, 'Don't worry about it, we'll sort it out from our end.'

'Well okay then,' said Julie, still looking puzzled.

Jack thanked her for her time and went back to his car. He was starting to suspect that whatever he was involved in must be pretty big. Some person or group was working very hard to cover something up and they were quite comfortable killing people. Jack wished that he had brought his pistol with him. ASIO agents were not authorized to carry weapons but he had purchased a small pistol in his private capacity. He even had a license for it. His surveillance work sometimes took him into undesirable places and the pistol was for his protection, not for making arrests.

There was one remaining lead he could follow while in Adelaide. Jack's previous work experiences in this city had helped him to get to know the place but he had not previously dealt with the Royal Flying Doctors. Fortunately the car he had hired came equipped with a GPS navigator, so he used it to set a course for RFD's local base.

Jack drove along Victoria lane until he saw a small sign marking the entrance to the Royal Flying Doctors parking area. He found an empty parking bay conveniently situated in the shade of a tree. Adelaide was hot today, really hot, so it was best to avoid the sun as much as possible.

Once inside, he went to the reception desk and identified himself as detective Brown.

'And how can we help you today detective?' asked the pretty receptionist.

'I have some questions about a body or person your company flew in from the outback last week,' said Jack.

'Hold on,' she said in a sing-song voice, then spoke briefly to someone else on the phone.' Marcia will be with you in a sec.'

'Thank you,' said Jack and turned expectantly, waiting for someone to approach him. A few seconds later a curly-haired woman stepped through a door and said 'This way detective.'

Jack went into her office and sat down.

'I understand you want to know about the fella we brought in last week?' she asked.

'Yes, that's correct, apparently he was DOA?' asked Jack.

'It's possible,' said Marcia. 'But let me check the record.' She typed on her keyboard, hesitated, typed some more, then turned to Jack, looking pleased with herself, 'He was alive but critical when we picked him up. He's not listed as having died on the flight.'

'So he died on route to hospital?' asked Jack.

'I don't have that information,' said Marcia. 'Our responsibility ends at the point of hand over. SA ambulance would have an admin trail after that.'

'Okay, I'll check with them,' said Jack. 'Do you have his name and address perhaps?'

'Yes, his name was Melnik Stapels. His address is listed as Oak Valley.'

'Where the bloody hell is that?'

Marcia laughed and said, 'It's a small community out in the Maralinga area, about 1000 kilometers away from here.'

'It can't be that small if they have an airport,' said Jack, thinking of the RFD aeroplane.

'There is no airport,' said Marcia. 'We use a small airfield 16 kilometers from the community.'

'Do you know if there is a commercial service going that way?'

'I doubt it, it's restricted airspace. We have special permission to fly in there weekly.'

'Why is it restricted?' asked Jack.

'I'm not sure, something to do with the military or the Air Force using the area.'

Jack looked dismal, he needed to get there but it was starting to look impossible. He could use his Federal or ASIO fake identities to get the necessary permissions, but that would draw too much attention. Marcia sensed Jack's conundrum it seemed, because she said, 'Our weekly flight leaves tomorrow morning. I can get you on board… but fair warning, it's going to be a very cramped and uncomfortable few hours for you.'

Jack could have hugged her but opted for a more professional response and said, 'Yes, that would be much faster. I was dreading all the paperwork I would have to go through to get a Federal plane out there.'

'Okay, they take off at 7.30 AM. I'll let them know to expect you.'

Marcia gave Jack instructions on how to reach the RFD hangar at Adelaide Airport. He would not be following the usual airport check in procedures. Jack thanked her and left.

He now had to find a room for the night and he was getting hungry. He also had a lot to think about. Melnik it seemed, had encountered a source of radiation on land which was owned or controlled by the government. It was also entirely possible that someone posing as SA ambulance personal had somehow put an early end to Melnik's misery, to prevent him from telling anyone where he had been when he got sick. Another thought occurred to him. He was going to the outback. He had better go and find an outdoor shop and pick up some suitable gear. It was quite possible that he may end up doing some hiking and camping in the bush for several days before finding what he was looking for.

Jack was on his way to meet the RFD plane. Earlier that morning, he had logged into the secure chat server and written up what he had discovered the previous day. He also added that he was going to Oak Valley and was unsure of how long he would be there.

He found the RFD hangar just as Marcia had described it, complete with parking area for his car. He then phoned Avis and told them that he was leaving the car just around the corner from them with the keys in the ignition. A young male doctor and a slightly older female nurse were standing at the loading door of the Pilatus PC12, a small single engined plane used by RFD in South Australia.

They appeared to be loading a number of small bags and boxes into the plane. Jack made sure that he was wearing his gold and red Federal badge and then walked up to them in a friendly and confident manner. 'Hello! I'm Paul Brown. I believe you guys are expecting me.'

The male doctor looked up, smiled and extended his hand saying, 'Hi Paul, yes, Marcia filled us in. I'm Tom...' He then jerked his head in the nurses direction and said, 'Anne.'

Anne shot a glance at Jack's empty ring finger as she extended her hand then said cheerfully, 'Hello, I'm Anne. I'm so glad to have you along.' She bent down and picked up a box, making sure her ample behind was pointed in Jack's direction. Jack winced, he was not looking forward to this trip. Anne continued talking as they loaded the last few items onto the plane. At one point Jack gave Tom a questioning look but Tom only managed a small tight-lipped smile.

Jack climbed in last and sat near the loading door then their pilot, Andrew, taxied out onto the runway.

Chapter 6

Jack had managed to put a dampener on Anne's advances by talking about his 'girlfriend' Renae. They were not in any agreed upon relationship but had grown closer as they got to know each other the night that Jack spent on the couch. He had told Renae about his family, their involvement in the field of the arts, and his childhood in Japan. They had shared a laugh when it was discovered that Renae owned one of Jill's CD's. Jack had discovered that Renae was an only child whose parents both worked in the finance industry.

From time to time Jack watched the passing landscape below him. They had flown out over St Vincent Gulf followed by Spencer Gulf and then the green began to fade rapidly as the land dried up. Tom pointed out various places of interest along the way such has the huge salt lakes of Lake Acraman. This dry lake bed was apparently the result of a huge meteorite impact hundreds of millions of years ago.

Eventually the plane began to descend and Jack did his best imitation of a kid and asked 'Are we there yet?' Anne and Tom had a good laugh but then Tom said 'No, we need to refuel so we are landing at Ceduna.' *Damn* thought Jack, *Australia was a bloody big place.* At least he could get out and stretch his legs a bit. He could also use a trip to the toilet.

Ceduna airport was a disappointment to Jack. He was used to the opulence of Sydney and this place seemed sparse and flat for miles in all directions. As they were coming in for the landing, he had seen the town and ocean in the distance and that had looked more welcoming then where there were now. The airfield was surrounded by farm lands and there was a warm, earthy smell in the air.

Forty minutes later they were ready to depart again. After take off the plane headed due west for some time before turning north. The land below became rapidly drier as they went further north and the general color of the landscape became orange brown. Jack could also see a long thin stripe stretching off to the horizon. According to Anne it was the *Trans Continental Railway* which had a famous passenger train called the *Indian Pacific Express* which traveled the full width of the continent from Perth to Sydney. She had taken that trip four years ago and shared some of the highlights with Jack and Tom. Jack was fascinated and it occurred to him that it might be a good experience to take Renae on that train trip one day.

After what felt like forever, the plane started to descend once more. Jack looked out the windows to try to see where they were headed. He was surprised to see a long straight dirt road and next to it, a brown airstrip carved out of the very earth it seemed. Near the end of the runway was a solitary building made of corrugated iron. It seemed just large enough to accommodate the plane they were in. Apart from that there was nothing other than miles and miles of brown earth mixed with sparse green vegetation. *How did people survive out here,* thought Jack.

The landing was much smoother than Jack had expected considering that it was a dirt runway. The plane then taxied to the metallic building before stopping. Jack was first out the door and it felt as if he had just walked into a brick wall of heat. This was a very dry heat with very little, if any, humidity. He estimated the temperature to be around 40° C. Anne and Tom climbed out next and then appeared to braced themselves for the heat. They were clearly expecting it. Jack also noticed how quiet it was. The persistent drone of the aeroplane engines had ceased, but it was more than that. There were no city noises, no cars, no hooters, no noisy people. Only the occasional bird sound broke the silence. Jack felt as if he somehow had more space, or perhaps it was a feeling of space being more freely available, one no longer had to compete for it. It was just there for the taking. It was a feeling of relief.

Just then a vehicle arrived seemingly out of nowhere. It was an old four-wheel drive of some sort and Jack did not recognize the make or model. It was covered in dust. The driver, a cheerful Aboriginal man in his mid forties climbed out and walked over to them. He nodded his head at the other two then extended his hand to Jack and said 'You be a stranger here, I'm Lenny.'

'Paul,' said Jack smiling.

Lenny opened the rear doors of his vehicle and started loading some medical supplies from the plane. Jack helped him with loading some boxes and was pleased to notice the cooler air at the back of the vehicle.

'You got air conditioning!' said Jack, seeming surprised.

Lenny looked pleased and said, 'Yes, she's old but she's good.' He looked at Jack curiously and added, 'You're not from the medical mob?'

'No,' said Jack. 'I'm here to figure out what happened to Melnick Staples. Did you know him?'

'Of course,' said Lenny, 'We all know each other. We only 100 people or so out at our place.'

'Do you know how he got sick?' asked Jack.

'No, I only saw him sick. You best be speaking to Trevor, they were mates.'

They finished up loading Lenny's car and then everyone climbed in, relieved to be out of the heat. Lenny turned northwest on to the dirt road and then they drove the last 16 kilometers to the clinic at Oak Valley community.

###

Arriving at Oak Valley, Jack was surprised to see that there were no visible oak trees, nor were they in a valley. He assumed that perhaps the name was a mixture of good humor and wishful thinking. He did spot some eucalyptus trees which were much taller than the native shrubbery. Jack asked Lenny about the oak trees and he pointed out some dark green trees near the school. He said they were native Desert Oaks and apparently there were a few in the area.

Lenny parked outside the clinic and Anne and Tom went inside to go see some patients and the local nurse. Jack helped them carry some supplies inside and then Lenny took him to where Trevor was working on an old car at the local mechanics garage. After some brief introductions, Jack began asking questions about Melnick.

'I'm trying to find what it was that made Melnick sick,' said Jack. 'Is there anything that you can tell me about it?'

'The water delivery fella found his truck on the side of the road, some few k's before the airfield. Melnick was still in the car and very sick so the water fella bring him here. We nurse him as best we can but he gets sicker all the time. The medical mob also try an fix him until they take him away in the plane.'

'Where was he coming from?' asked Jack.

'He had been out a few days, setting and checking traps. Out on the east side of Lake Maurice. It was before Christmas you see. He was trying to get rabbits.'

'Are there any old mines out there?' asked Jack. 'We think that whatever made him sick was a man-made thing.'

'No... sometimes there are some mineral exploration fellas out there. They make holes in the ground, about as thick as my arm.'

'Do these people leave any chemicals around, empty tins and so on?'

'Nah, not that I can remember.'

'What about military stuff, old bombs or old containers?'

'Not where he was. There is an old army base a 100 k's further east. It's where this whole area got its name from you know, Maralinga, it means *the place of thunder*.'

'Do you think he would have gone there?'

'We all know not to go there. That nuclear stuff make you sick. After those bombs went off in the fifties, a black cloud blew over where my uncle was living. He come a blind after that.'

Jack was astounded. Did he hear correctly, *nuclear stuff*?

'What nuclear stuff?'

'You don't know?' asked Trevor, looking surprised. 'Government fellas were testing nuclear bombs out there in the old days. Many of us got crooked from that. They say it's all clean now but we don't believe them... we don't go there.'

Jack thought this over. There must surely be a connection between Melnick and the old nuclear test site. Melnick knew not to go there which meant that the problem had somehow found him.

'Is there a way we can retrace where he went?' asked Jack.

'I've been with him before, out there. I can follow his tracks that his truck make.'

It occurred to Jack that the radioactive material may also have contaminated Melnick's truck, so he asked, 'Where is Melnick's truck?'

'Its right here,' said Trevor and with an elegant motion of his hand, he gestured at the vehicle he was working on.

Oh shit! thought Jack. *He was standing right next to the damned thing.* He instinctively stepped back. He had set his wristwatch to start beeping if it detected any radiation that he should be worrying about. It had not beeped. He had no way of knowing if it even worked.

'Did Melnick bring anything back with him? Like sand or pieces of metal or anything unusual,' asked' asked Jack trying to sound calm.

'No... nothing like that, just a few rabbits and some leftover food and water.'

'What happened to it?' asked Jack, feeling some tension in the pit of the stomach.

'We had it for Christmas,' said Trevor, looking at Jack as if he had just asked a really stupid question.

Jack realized that it could not have been the rabbits, or more people would have died.

'What happened to the left over water?'

'It's still there in his water bottle,' said Trevor, then seeing that Jack was expecting more information he added, 'in my kitchen cupboards, under the sink.'

'It might be what poisoned him,' said Jack. 'I assume you have not had any.'

Trevor shook his head.

'I'll need to test it. I also want to make sure that this vehicle is not contaminated either.'

Jack started at the front of the vehicle and worked his way to the back, slowly scanning the wrist detector around the tires, wheel wells and sides of the truck. When he got to the back he was surprised to see the word Ford on the tailgate. He did the same test on the other side. Satisfied that the outside was safe he then opened the door and carefully checked inside, but it was also negative. Jack closed the door again just as Trevor arrived with a 5 liter plastic container. It still had a bit of water in it. Jack scanned it with his wrist detector and got a positive reading as well as several consecutive beeps.

'What's that mean?' asked Trevor, referring to the beeps.

'It means that this is what killed Melnick'. Jack looked Trevor in the eye and said, 'It's really important that we find out where Melnick's got this water.'

'He woulda taken water with him but if he was running low out there then he woulda found some desert water.'

'What do you mean?' asked Jack. He was thinking that maybe the ground water had become contaminated.

'You find water in low shady places sometimes, like at the bottom of some rocks where the sun don't shine. Rain water can collect there and it stay there for a few weeks after sometimes.'

Trevor was still holding the water container. He looked down at it suspiciously and asked, 'Is it safe to be near the stuff?'

Jack knew that the small amount of gamma radiation coming out of the water was not the real problem. The water was probably contaminated with radioactive particles emitting much heavier alpha and beta radiation. That types of radiation did not travel through the air and was only harmful if the actual particles were inhaled or ingested. Once they were in the body they would start destroying cells quite rapidly.

Jack tried to simplify it for Trevor and said, 'It's safe at that distance but you don't want to drink it or sleep with it under your pillow. I think it's best if we give it to the medical mob to take back with them and dispose of properly. We should also wash the outside off first to make sure there is no poison left on it.' Jack realized that with Trevor having handing the water container already, there was a chance that he may have come into contact with the radioactive particles, but he hoped that this was not the case.

'How soon can we go out and follow Melnick's trail.,' asked Jack.

'It be best if we left at sunrise tomorrow,' said Trevor.

Early next morning just as the sky was getting light, Jack and Trevor set out in yet another unrecognizable old four-wheel drive. Jack had spent the night on a bed in the clinic. There was not much space in Trevor's tiny house and the bed in the clinic was comfortable and going to waste. Jack had told the *medical mob* that he would be staying a few days. He would either find his own way back, or catch a ride with them again the following week.

They drove with the windows closed and did not do too much talking. Despite the hot midday temperatures, the morning air was quite chilly. The road noise inside the cab of the vehicle was so loud that it made speaking quite difficult. As they drove past the airfield Jack noticed that there was a fence running all the way around it. He asked Trevor what it was for and got told that it was there to keep the wildlife off the runway. Apparently there were camels, kangaroos and emus that would wander onto the airfield and cause all kinds of problems and delays when a plane wanted to land.

They drove another 24 kilometers beyond the airfield and then the road dipped into a large natural gulley before rising up the other side again. At the very top of this rise, Trevor pulled over to the side and stopped. The sun was now just creeping over the horizon and casting long shadows across the land. They got out of the truck and Trevor began searching for the spot where Melnick had driven out of the bush and joined the dirt road. After some time he found it and motioned for Jack to come over and take a look. The tracks appeared to be coming in from the North East and as Jack looked in that direction, the only thing he saw was a vast flat land of red earth intermingled with knee-high grass and an occasional green bush about the size of their vehicle.

'What's out there?' asked Jack.

'About ten k's north is Lake Maurice,' said Trevor and then beckoning North East with his right arm, he added. 'And out that way you will find a lot more of what you see in front of you now.'

Jack was feeling a bit overwhelmed by the vast size of the land but Trevor seemed to take it in his stride. They both returned to the truck and then Trevor began following Melnick's tracks, driving much slower this time.

The tracks continued going northwest for about ten kilometers and then they turned and headed off in a northerly direction. After about another ten kilometers they stopped in any area which showed signs of someone having made camp.

'He spent the night here,' said Trevor. Off in the far distance, Jack could see a large dry salt lake, huge in fact. The edges where the land met the lake were surprisingly steep. The lake bed itself appeared to be about twenty to thirty meters lower than the rest of the land surrounding it.

'Is there ever water in that?' asked Jack as he stared at the far off lake bed.

'I've seen it with water in but the salt make it useless.'

Jack pictured what it would look like full of water and then found himself feeling sad about it having no water in now. He imagined it looking like a large inland sea with sailing boats and holiday resorts around the outside. The temperature was knocking at 33° C and he was feeling hot and sticky. He would have loved an ocean to swim in right about then. It had taken them five hours to get this far and he was also hungry. They decided to break for lunch.

Sometime later they set off again. The tracks they were following were now heading southeast. It felt like they were crawling. A fit man could comfortably jog along beside them at the pace they were going. They drove for several more hours and the sun was beginning to get low, but it was just then that Jack saw something ahead. There was a glint of sunlight reflecting off a metallic object. As they drew closer, Melnick's tracks showed that he had stopped there. Jack cautioned Trevor to stay upwind of the object as they approached and then they parked about thirty meters away. Jack now recognized the object as being a scoop or bucket from a back-hoe. It was partly buried in the sand and covered in dust.

Back-hoe bucket

'How did that get here?' asked Jack.

'I only see Melnick's tracks,' said Trevor. 'Mind you, we had a big one blow through here a few months back. It woulda covered any tracks.'

'A big what... '

'Dust storm, real bad one.'

They sat for a few moments longer and then Jack said 'Wait here... I need to check if its been contaminated.'

He climbed out the vehicle and approached cautiously with his wristwatch as far out ahead of him as he could get it. He got to within two meters of the bucket before his watch started beeping. Jack stopped and examined the scene from where he was. The bucket was positioned so that the concave portion was facing upwards and some rain water had collected in it.

He could also see that the teeth on the edge of the bucket were caked with some type of clay or soil. Some of this had washed off and collected in the base of the bucket. Melnick had probably collected water from here, not realizing that this back-hoe had dug in radioactive soil. Jack turned around and went back to the vehicle.

Trevor could see that Jack was troubled by something.

'Is that thing radioactive?' he asked.

'Unfortunately it is, and some rain water has collected in it.'

They both remained silent for a few moments. Trevor was thinking about his friend Melnick. The week before Christmas was unusually hot and Melnick's must have needed more water than he had with him. Jack was thinking about the bigger picture. He was just beginning to see what this was all about. Someone had taken a back-hoe and had managed to dig up some radioactive material, most likely from the Maralinga test site. There was only one possible reason that he could think of. Someone was building a dirty bomb, maybe even several dirty bombs, depending on how much radioactive material they had managed to get. Whoever they were, they were well-connected and had killed many people to keep their secret.

'How do we get into that Maralinga test site?' asked Jack.

'We'll have to turn south and keep going until we reach Lake Dey Dey road. From there it's another forty kilometers to the main gate. We won't make it today. We make camp somewhere and go in the morning.'

'Okay but let's put some distance between us and this thing,' said Jack. They drove south through the bush for a while and then set up camp for the night. Jack had wanted to leave an update on the secure server but there was no mobile phone reception for hundreds of kilometers around.

They ate snake for breakfast. A big brown snake had entered the camp the previous night. Trevor had clubbed it with a stick and then hung it in a thorn tree. Jack had not even seen the snake, he just saw Trevor jump up, grab a sturdy stick and chase something. Whatever it was, it was fast because Trevor had to actually run to keep up with it. A while later he returned with the snake draped over the end of the stick. They both slept in the vehicle that night.

Jack was no fan of weird food. They still had rabbit sandwiches in the vehicle and he was content to eat that rather than snake, but once the snake was cooking over the fire it actually smelt quite good. When he dared to taste some he discovered that it actually tasted like chicken, not *exactly* like chicken but it was white meat and tasted good enough.

They broke camp and set off soon afterward. After about another hour of slow driving through the bush they eventually joined Lake Dey Dey road and turned left, heading for Maralinga Village. It was a relief to be back on the dirt roads and they covered the remaining forty kilometers in record time.

The entrance to the village was blocked by two big metal gates on which was posted two big stop signs, a Chevron and several other warning signs. There was also a blue and white sign advising them to call ahead and ask for assistance. On the left hand side of the gate was what looked like a really old telephone box. Painted across the top were the words *The Tardis*. He figured that the pill-box shaped phone booth might be the actual one that the British installed during the 1950s. Jack then went and used the field telephone in the phone booth and spoke to someone called William who told him that he would send his assistant to let them in.

Jack and Trevor were escorted to a small office where they met up with William, a white bloke with grey hair.

'Hello mates, what brings you out to our scratch in the sand?' he asked.

Jack had already told him via the gate phone that he was a Federal detective, so he went ahead and said, 'We found a piece of a back-hoe about thirty kilometers northwest of here. The evidence suggests that it was used for digging in soil that was radioactive...' Jack paused long enough to make sure that William was following him and then he continued, 'Have you seen any fresh holes out at the old test sites?'

'Mate, this area where the testing was done spreads about forty kilometers by forty kilometers. It's a huge piece of sand. I drive up there once a week or so and throw my eyes around a bit, but I ain't seen anything out-of-place,' said William.

'What type of security do you guys have out here?' asked Jack, trying not to sound as if he was accusing him of anything. He had expected to see a military base, with soldiers and jeeps and tanks, or perhaps a few helicopters, but instead this place was a ghost town.

'Well it's fenced off mate,' said William. 'What more do you want. We are in a no fly zone in the middle of nowhere.'

Jack was beginning to see the attitude that the government had towards this place. They had exploded various nuclear weapons over a period of about ten years. Then the cleanup began which consisted of scraping off the top layer of soil and burying it in large trenches. They then put a fence around the place and patted themselves on their backs for a job well done. Security consisted of an old couple who were caretaker's of the historical village.

Jack was about to ask the old guy if they could drive up there and take a look around, but he had second thoughts. The wind only had to kick up a single particle of radioactive material and if he inhaled it, he could very well be dying of leukemia at a later date.

William could see that Jack was wrestling with the problem of finding freshly dug holes, so he said, 'Why don't you ask the *Outback Mineral Exploration* pilot to fly you around in his chopper. You may also want to check out the Emu Fields area.'

'You have a chopper here?' asked Jack hopefully.

'Not me, but *Outback Mineral Exploration* have one down at the airfield.'

'What airfield?' asked Jack, feeling really stupid.

William realized that Jack knew little to nothing about the area. 'There's an airfield about two or three kilometers from here. The Air Force were flying in a lot of people and equipment back in the heyday.'

'That sounds good,' said Jack. 'What was that about Emu Fields?'

'That's where the first rounds of nuclear testing was done. It's about 150 kilometers North East of here. The British then decided that it was too far from the railway line, so they set up this site here at Maralinga.'

'Was there any radioactive material buried out there as well?' asked Jack.

'Same as here,' said William. 'They scraped the top layer off and then buried it.'

'I must admit that I'm quite shocked,' said Jack. 'Anyone with the right equipment can come out here and help themselves to nuclear waste material.'

'But only an idiot would go near the stuff,' said William.

'The are a lot of idiots who would be happy to die for their cause,' countered Jack.

William just shrugged and said, 'So, do you want to speak to the pilot or not?'

'Yes please, if you can tell you where to find him.'

The pilot's name was Adam and he had agreed to fly Jack and Trevor around, for a price of course. Trevor had never flown in anything before and he was quite excited, if not a little bit scared. They had found Adam next to a water pool under some trees near the west runway. It was like a mini oasis.

Adam explained that the British had designed the runway with a slight curved surface so that rain water would run off and collect in channels on either side of the runway. From there the water was redirected to this rock pool which had served as the main water supply for the people at the village. It held 1.8 million liters of water. Jack thought it was ingenious. The actual runway was equally impressive. This was not an airfield, it was a proper airport with a reinforced sealed surfaces. In its day, large military cargo aircraft had landed here filled with equipped and people, many of whom were prominent scientist. Nearly 3000 people had apparently lived and worked at the village that William now looked after.

They walked the short distance from the water pool to where the helicopter was parked on the side apron, next to a fuel tanker. Jack questioned Adam about his duties as the helicopter pilot.

'Why does a mineral exploration company need a helicopter out here?' asked Jack.

'We have guys in the field who drive and operate small drilling rigs used for obtaining core samples. It's too far and too time consuming for them to drive back here every morning and every night. So my main job is to play air taxi.'

'So your field people live here in the village?'

'Yeah, it's far more comfortable than camping in the bush.'

'Have you seen any unusual activity out here in the last few months?'

'In the village?'

'More in the out back, or did something unusual happened in the village?'

'No, I can't say that I have seen anything unusual. Life is quite simple out here.'

'So this is your helicopter,' said Jack as a gleaming white Bell Jetranger 206 helicopter came into view. 'I kind of expected it to be full of dust, like Trevor's car.'

Adam and Trevor laughed then Adam said, 'I like to keep it spotless, it gives me something to do in between flights and it forces me to get up close and personal and spot any possible problems.'

'You guys can go ahead and climb in. I just need to pull the dust covers off the jet ports.'

'Why don't you sit in front,' said Jack to Trevor.

'No, no, not me, I'd rather sit in the back,' said Trevor looking terrified.

As they rose up in the air, Jack was able to see the Airport in all its glory. The runway seemed to go on for ever.

'How long is that runaway?' asked Jack.

'Its two kilometers long,' said Adam. 'Apparently it's the only runway in Australia where the space shuttle could land in an emergency. I'll show you what the village looks like from up here.' Adam flew west towards the historical village and then slowly circled around the south-west end of it, giving Jack and Trevor and excellent view of the village.

'Wow, there is even a swimming pool there,' said Jack.

'Yeah, it gets used a lot. Very thoughtful of the British,' said Adam.

'Why are they so many vacant lots, it looks like there were buildings on them,' asked Jack.

'That's true,' said Adam. 'Many of the original buildings were sold off to farmers and towns in the area. Apparently there were some well made aluminum sheds and a church among the things that were sold. Now that the land has been returned to the Anangu people, there is some talk of recovering and restoring all the buildings that were here, for a... uhm a tourist attraction type thing. It would be a way for the Anangu people to earn some money.'

'So the land is no longer controlled by the government?' asked Jack, concerned about the security of the nuclear waste.

'I am not sure how that works,' said Adam.

Jack felt confused. Surely the government was not passing the problem on to the Anangu people. *You wanted the land now deal with the waste*. Or was the hand over purely symbolic? Were the Anangu people now responsible for the security of the area? That would be ridiculous. Surely all the buried nuclear material should be under constant military guard.

Adam started flying north and Jack noticed a few other peculiarities. The land below was full of scratchings and areas where the ground had been scraped. There were many dirt roads that would end abruptly for no apparent reason. They flew past an oval which had perhaps been used for racing or exercise in the past. Beyond that was another area where the ground had been disturbed. Who knew what had gone on there or what was buried beneath it. They were only 1.5 kilometers from the village but there was evidence on the ground of explosive detonations. Jack figured that they could not have been nuclear explosions simply because it would have wiped out the village at such a close distance.

Adam flew northwest along a road for another seventeen kilometers and then the road split up into three main sections which in turn split up into smaller arteries. At the end of these arteries were more blast sites which Adam confirmed as being the sites where the nuclear tests were done. Jack was shocked. He was looking for evidence of ground being disturbed, but it was an impossible mission. All along the roads he had seen burial pits, trenches and scrapings numbering in the hundreds. There would be no way to tell if anyone had removed material and covered their tracks. The northwestern blast site must have been the worst because it had a vast area from which the top soil had been scraped clean. Along the western edge were too long rows of burial pits in which the most radioactive material had been placed. Most alarming to Jack was the fact that even sixty years after the event there were still no trees growing anywhere in the area.

'The Emu Fields test sites are another 150 kilometers northwest of here,' said Adam.

'May as well take a look,' said Jack, feeling miserable.

The Emu Fields test sites were vastly different to the Maralinga site. Here there was little to no evidence of a big clean up. There was no evidence of the top soil having been removed and there appeared to be two long trenches alongside the roads which led up to the two detonation sites. Once again Jack concluded that it was impossible to determine if anyone had removed waste material from the site. There were also no trees growing in the area, only some very short grass and weeds.

'William said that there was an airfield out here as well,' said Jack, looking around.

'Yes,' said Adam. 'It is just to the northwest of here.'

Adam took them to where the airfield was. It was a dirt runway similar to the one at Oak Valley but much longer. Jack estimated it to be about 1.8 kilometers long and it appeared to be in perfect condition. An impressive testament to the people who built it sixty years ago. Jack considered what he had learnt so far. A back-hoe had been used to dig up nuclear material. How did it get here? How was it removed and disposed of? They had dropped the scoop-bucket belonging to the back-hoe, probably a safety precaution. The Emu Fields test site was deserted but it had a runaway where a big cargo plane could have been used to transport the back-hoe and the radioactive material, however it was a big risk. The air space here was monitored from Woomera air force base and a big cargo plane would be very noticeable.

Jack decided that the back-hoe must have been brought in by land, it would have been the least conspicuous method. The only roads that a flat-bed truck could travel on were down at Oak Valley which meant that the back-hoe must have arrived and departed from there. He recalled that the Transcontinental Railway line was ten kilometers to the south of Maralinga village. If he, Jack, were going to transport radioactive material, he would put it on a goods train and not risk police checks and other random events which could occur along a road.

Jack turned around and looking at Trevor, asked, 'What's the closest train station to Maralinga village?'

'That be Watson,' said Trevor.

'Let's go there,' said Jack.

###

Adams flew in low over Watson station. It did not really qualify as a station, at least not to a city boy like Jack. There was no platform but there were a few out buildings and a small community amounting to eight houses.

'Do trains really stop here?' asked Jack.

'Yes said Adam. We bring in heavyweight equipment and spare parts via this station.'

'Can we land somewhere?' asked Jack. 'I want to question the people who live here.'

'You realize I am going to get dust all over my nice clean helicopter,' said Adam.

'Yeah, yeah, we both know you won't be cleaning it again until tomorrow morning anyway,' said Jack.

Adam circled around a few times and Jack realized that he was looking for a landing spot that would kick up the least amount of dust.

'How about there,' said Jack, indicating an area which had been scraped clean down to bedrock.

'Yeah, that will do,' said Adam and then he carefully landed the helicopter at the location.

Jack and Trevor climbed out and crouch walked under the spinning rotor blades towards the nearby settlement. A few happy dogs ran up to greet them, barking and wagging their tails. Not too far behind them, some Aboriginal children were also running towards them. Jack waved at the children and then bent down and patted the dogs.

Jack had learned not to be dismissive of children. They were often out and about playing in areas that adults never went to, and as a result, they often saw and noticed things that adults were not aware of. They could provide useful intelligence.

Jack spent some time chatting to the kids, making them feel important, which encouraged them to trust him with the information they had. They also appreciated that he seemed to like what they liked, namely their dogs. Before long he learnt that one of them had seen a back-hoe being loaded on to a flat-bed rail carriage at night.

It had happened nearly three months earlier during a big dust storm which had woken the child and made him look outside. What was interesting was that the back-hoe had not arrived on a truck, nor had it come down the road to the station. The child said that the back-hoe had come from the northwest, straight out of the desert.

Upon further questioning, he also revealed that the front loader section was carrying several large fuel drums. The train had stopped as the back-hoe had arrived and then they had simply driven the back-hoe on to the flatbed carriage and then the train departed again, heading east towards Sydney. No one had climbed off the carriage.

They had remained with the vehicle when the train departed. None of this struck Jack as being normal behavior.

By now two adults had also arrived so Jack question them as well. They could not give any more information but Jack learnt that a goods train would be stopping here in two hours time. He walked Trevor back to the waiting helicopter and told them to go back without him. He was going to stow away aboard the goods strain and get back to Sydney that way.

Chapter 7

Three months earlier.

New Holland B115B - Back-hoe - front loader

Golakov was busy modifying the New Holland B115B back-hoe which they had bought secondhand from a government yard in Perth. His boss had no shortage of money but they could not risk contracting this job out. The modifications were too unusual and might attract unwanted attention.

The task at hand was to insert a three stage HEPA air filter in line with an air compressor to pressurize the back-hoe cabin. This would allow them to work in a cloud of radioactive dust without the risk of inhaling any lethal particles. Todorova had suggested that it might be easier to just hire a local Aboriginal to go dig out the radioactive material at Maralinga and then shoot him when the job was done. He said that they were too stupid to know that the dust would kill them. It would be simpler than doing all this work to modify the back-hoe. The problem with that plan, according to Golakov, was that you could not trust the Aboriginal to get the job done right. Golakov also knew where the really potent radioactive material was buried and he had to make sure that they got some of that stuff. Besides, Golakov could not bring himself to trust anyone. He did not even trust Todorova with the work of pressurizing the cabin. He had assigned Todorova the task of fitting explosive bolts to the back-hoe rear scoop. If he screwed it up, it was his blood that would be spilt, not Golakov's.

Golakov never rushed. He took his time and measured everything very carefully. Measure twice, cut once was his motto. He took two full days to do the cabin modifications and when it was done, it was a robust work of art. It was also a very sturdy construction that would easily withstand several days of outback riding through the bush. He also checked Todorova's work on the rear scoop and decided that it was adequate. Next he carefully affixed some large stickers to the sides of the back-hoe. The wording on the stickers read *Outback Mineral Exploration*.

Finally, he loaded six 44 gallon drums into the front loading bucket of the machine. These drums had been modified with an inner lead lining and had been filled with diesel fuel.

Golakov then drove the back-hoe on to a flat-bed train carriage, tied it down and covered it with a tarpaulin. Their boss had rented them a workshop in an industrial area which had its own train line next to it. That night, a diesel locomotives had come up the train line and hauled away the carriage to make it part of a goods train headed for Sydney.

Golakov and Todorova were waiting at Oldea station for the goods train to arrive. They had chosen the station because, it was the closest one to the Maralinga site, with a dirt runway right next to the railway line. This particular runway was just outside of the no fly zone. A low flying light aircraft had landed there at night and dropped them off along with backpacks and weapons. The entire operation had been timed to coincide with an approaching storm and they had two days to get into position before the storm hit.

The station was not an official stop on the transcontinental line and there was no community living here. In the past it had been used for off loading mining equipment and the occasional special request. Today's stop was a special request filed under the name of the

Outback Mineral Exploration company. They sometimes off loaded equipment here which was convenient for Golakov for using as a cover. He and Todorova also wore shirts with the company logo on.

Golakov also carried a small two-way radio which operated on the same frequency used by the railway. As the train came within range, the train driver radioed ahead to Golakov to confirm that he had to stop. This was how the *Outback Mineral Exploration* did business in the area.

Golakov confirmed that they wanted to off load equipment, and several minutes later the train came into view, and slowed down, ready to halt. Golakov waved at the train driver as he passed and then they collaborated via radio to bring the train to a stop in a position where the flat-bed carriage was next to a raised embankment. Golakov and Todorova then unchained the back-hoe, removed the tarpaulin and drove the machine on to the raised embankment next to the carriage. They advised the train driver that he was good to go and then they drove off in the direction of the runway, to where they had stashed their gear.

From there they went due north, not bothering with roads. Golakov had specifically chosen this model back-hoe because it had large front wheels and could travel cross-country at a fairly rapid rate. They drove for forty kilometers and then Golakov used their German-made military GPS navigator to guide them to their campsite, where they parked the back-hoe among some trees and covered it in camouflage netting.

The sky was purple and bruised as if it had done battle with a mighty warrior. A fierce wind was also blowing, causing trees to lean over and shake their branches in protest. It would rain later but for now the land was dry and a fine dust filled the air.

It would be dark soon and Golakov was preparing to leave. He and Todorova were busy removing the camouflage netting and doing battle with the wind which kept turning and twisting the net and thwarting their efforts as they fought to remove it.

Eventually they freed the net and it was immediately swept away in a cloud of dust only to get tangled in another tree. Golakov had earlier used a hand pump to extract diesel fuel from the 44 gallon drums and fill the tanks of the vehicle. He went around to the front loader section and rechecked the drums they had stacked inside the massive front bucket. Those drums were vital for the next part of the plan and he was not going to lose them to the weather.

Thirty minutes later they climbed into the cabin and started the engine. Golakov was wearing passive night vision goggles which allowed him to drive in the dark without the use of the vehicles lights. Todorova wore a similar pair. His main job was to deal with any unwanted guests and kill them quietly. They did not want any witnesses to what they were about to do.

They drove in silence at low-speed with Golakov occasionally checking the GPS to make sure he was on track to the dig site. It took them and hour to cover the last ten kilometers before arriving at the boundary fence. Golakov simply pushed it over and drove on. In weather like this one would expect the occasional tree and fence section to get blown over. After another ten minutes they stopped at the place Golakov had chosen.

Golakov lowered the front loader bucket on to the ground and then they both got out and braved the wind to remove the six 44 gallon drums from the bucket. This was done by tipping the drums slightly to one side and then rolling them out to form a single line with the drums spaced about one meter apart. Todorova now removed the top lead-lined covers of the drums and then lay the drums on their sides one at a time to allow the last of the diesel fuel to drain out before standing them upright again.

The drums were now ready to receive their lethal load. They climbed back into the vehicle cabin then Golakov began operating the controls of the back-hoe. He dug a five meter long trench, by three meters deep, throwing the dirt on the ground to one side. Next he dug further down but this time he carefully placed the dirt into the drums which he had lined up next to the trench. Once the drums were full he refilled the trench with the dirt he had discarded to the side.

Next came the tricky part. Golakov drove the vehicle a short distance upwind of where they had dug the trench and then Todorova donned a plastic hazardous materials suit and breathing apparatus. He left the vehicle cabin and walked back to the filled in trench where he replaced the covers on the drums. Golakov brought the vehicle around and positioned it so that Todorova could roll the drums back in to the front loader bucket.

When he had done so, Golakov moved the vehicle upwind of the trench again. Here he dug a single hole with one scoop of the back-hoe bucket and waited for Todorova to throw his hazardous materials suit and breathing apparatus into the hole. Todorova then climbed back into the vehicle cabin and Golakov closed up the hole he had dug. The storm continued howling and wind-blown sand quickly filled in any evidence of them ever having been there.

Golakov exited the boundary fence at the same place where he had come in and then drove west. As a precaution he had not wanted to return the way they came, choosing instead a circular route which would first take them within twenty kilometers of Lake Maurice before heading southeast to the railway station at Watson. Along the way Golakov activated the explosive bolts on the back-hoe bucket, causing it to drop into the desert sand. It had been in contact with the radioactive material and this was the quickest and easiest way of getting rid of it.

When they were close to Watson, Golakov checked the time and saw that they were forty minutes early for the train so he parked the vehicle about one kilometer from the station and switched on his two-way radio. He had tried to adjust the pace of their journey through the desert so that his arrival here would coincide with the arrival of the train.

Sometime later, his radio crackled to life as the train driver informed the station attendants of his impending arrival. Golakov advised the train driver that he would be collaborating with them about loading a vehicle onto a flatbed carriage.

Golakov drove the back-hoe onto the flat-bed carriage and then he and Todorova secured it to the carriage with chains. On the far end of the carriage under a tarpaulin was a spare back-hoe bucket. They had also previously prepared this carriage back at the Perth workshop in the same way they had prepared the carriage which brought the New Holland B115B.

When the vehicle was secure, Golakov radioed the driver and informed him that they were ready to go. A short while later the train began to move, the driver unaware that the two men had remained on the carriage.

Once they were on the way, Golakov got busy with attaching the spare back-hoe bucket to the vehicle whilst Todorova removed the mineral exploration stickers. The task was made all the more difficult by the rocking of the carriage, the severe weather and the lack of light. No sooner was he done when it began to rain. He joined Todorova in the vehicle cabin where they remained until early the next morning when the train pulled into Tarcoola station.

Tarcoola had a small community with a small airport situated ten minutes walking distance away.

At the Airport, a single engined Cessna was waiting to pick them up.

Chapter 8

Jack lay on his back staring up at the stars as the train made its way through the great southern desert. He needed to update Randy with the latest information but there were no cell towers anywhere in range. He had strong doubts as to whether he would actually get into range of a cell tower until he reached Port Augusta. There was nothing to do but wait. He had found a cosy spot for himself just behind a large crate which shielded him from the wind. Not that he minded the wind too much, it was a warm 30° C and the bit of wind that made it around the crate was quite welcome.

He had considered going back to Maralinga Village with Adam and using their Internet connection to leave a message for Randy, but that meant that he would be putting the people at the village at risk. If his enemies had breached the security of the server then they could easily trace the IP address back to Williams computer. Jack thought about Renae, he missed her, especially the breakfast she had cooked for him. He had not eaten since this morning because they had taken the helicopter ride before lunch and then that afternoon they had gone straight to Watson and two hours later he had boarded the train.

As far as the people at Watson were concerned, he had returned to Maralinga. They had seen him climb into the back of the helicopter and then saw the helicopter take off. They had not seen him climb out the other side of the helicopter and hide behind some rocks before it took off. The massive dust cloud kicked up by the rotors made sure of that. Perhaps it was overkill, but he had to consider the fact that if the back-hoe had been loaded there, then one of the locals might be friendly with his enemies and he preferred them not knowing where he was.

Once everybody had returned to their homes he had carefully made his way to the southern side of the railway line and concealed himself there to await the train. His reason for doing that was so that the train would be between him and any on lookers at the settlement when he snuck aboard.

Jack figured that the drums the kid had seen on the front loader bucket of the vehicle was probably where they had put the nuclear material which they had dug up. If someone was building a dirty bomb it was probably intended for maximum destruction, which meant a big city. There were four major cities to the east, the biggest being Sydney. But that did not rule out the other three, Melbourne, Adelaide and Brisbane were still at risk. And what about Canberra, the political capital of Australia. That could also be the intended target.

He had to narrow it down. He would update Randy at the earliest opportunity so that he could use the railway database and try to find where the back-hoe had been off loaded. In fact, try to *find* was not acceptable, they absolutely **had** to find where it had been off loaded if they were going to find the radioactive material before someone used it in a bomb.

Early next morning Jack smelt a sea breeze and then looking ahead to the south he saw the lights of a small city or town. It had to be Port Augusta. He checked his mobile phone and much to his delight he saw that he had a weak signal. He used the browser app on his phone to log into the secure server and began to dictate his urgent update to Randy.

Sometime later, a change in the sound up ahead drew his attention away from what he was doing. He poked his head out past the crate and realized that they were crossing a train bridge. Looking out across the landscape in the weak morning light he saw the Eyre Peninsula to his south.

The train had now stopped going east end was now headed south, following the eastern bank of the Eyre Peninsula until it entered the northern section of Port Augusta. Jack continued dictating until finally, he posted his message and logged out just as the train ground to a halt in the train yard. There was probably going to be a few minutes of carriage switching and shunting before the train continued.

Jack considered his next move. He knew that Port Augusta had a small airport but there were no direct flights from there to Sydney. Port Augusta was 300 kilometers from Adelaide. If he remained on board the train it would take another three to four hours to get there. If he got off at Port Augusta and went in search of a rental car, it would still be about three to four hours before he got to Adelaide, but it would give him an opportunity to have breakfast, and he was hungry, very hungry.

Jack checked his watch and saw that it was 5.15 AM which meant that it was far too early to get breakfast or rent a car. It was also pointless trying to head straight to Sydney until he received a response from Randy. For all he knew, the back-hoe could have gone to Adelaide. He may as well stay on the train and he was going to have to stay hungry until the train got to Adelaide.

Fifteen minutes before the train pulled into the shunt yard in Adelaide, Jack checked the secure server and found a response from Randy. The railway database contained no record of a back-hoe vehicle being loaded in Watson on the night of the storm. Randy had dug deeper and discovered that there was a flatbed carriage carrying a back-hoe bucket on that night. There was no other cargo listed for that flat-bed carriage which seemed a bit strange given the amount of carriage space going to waste. The flatbed carrying the back-hoe bucket was listed as having been attached in Perth and detached from the train in Lithgow and was apparently still there.

Jack was convinced it had to be what they where looking for. Their back-hoe vehicle had abandoned its rear bucket out in the desert and it would have needed a replacement bucket. How convenient it was that on that very night, a flatbed carriage carrying nothing but a back-hoe bucket had stopped in Watson. There was ample space left on that carriage to park a back-hoe vehicle. It was clever of *them* to do it this way because it left no record of the vehicle being loaded and unloaded.

Jack left a new message on the server. It read, *I'm going to follow-up in Perth*. Randy would know that it was intentional misdirection and would take it to mean that he was headed for Lithgow. Jack now had to get to Lithgow which was 100 kilometers West of Sydney. The fastest way of getting there would be to take a flight from Adelaide to Sydney and then rent a car.

When the train finally stopped at the freight terminal in the Dudley Park suburb of Adelaide, Jack got off and climbed through a hole in the fence that took him to Regency Park where he found a taxi to take him to the airport. Once there, he bought a ticket to Sydney then went looking for a place to buy food, something *big* and tasty.

Jack had driven for nearly two hours. He had rented a four-wheel drive vehicle because he anticipated doing some off-road traveling, There were many farms and mines in the Lithgow area and most of them were accessed via dirt roads.

This rental car was top-heavy and not a good on-road performer. The road conditions were not that great either. The problem was that The Great Western Highway was only really great until it reached the top of the hill on the far Western fringe of Sydney. Beyond that it was a regular country road and was being constantly upgraded in various places.

The road was being widened so that cars could pass trucks on up hills and there was no shortage of hills. In fact, they were mountains, the Blue Mountains to be exact. The road constantly twisted and turned with the occasional revelation of a majestic view to the south. There were limited opportunities to pass other vehicles and it had been slow going for much of the time.

Eventually Jack saw a sign saying Katoomba and on impulse he turned left into the small town. It was 2:10 PM and he decided to break for lunch. He had been here before, a few years ago when he had visited the *Scenic Railway*, a popular tourist attraction featuring a narrow gauge train which during its last ninety meters went straight up the side of a cliff at a near vertical angle. He recalled that they served a decent lunch, not spectacular but at least it was better than a hamburger or a rabbit sandwich. He was only thirty kilometers from Lithgow which meant that if he ate quick and got moving again, he could be there by 3:00 PM at the latest.

Jack parked in the small parking garage next to the visitor center and noticed how full it was. He had forgotten that, being December, it was peak tourist season. The place was swarming with people. There was also two big tourist buses outside. Once inside, he bought his meal and then walked outside onto the deck to stand and eat it and enjoy the spectacular view across the valley.

An advert on the wall caught his attention. Katoomba airfield had twice daily flights to Sydney. He had not known that. It might have saved him time getting here but then he would have been stuck without a car when he got here. Nice to know anyway. Jack ate the last of his meal while watching tourists filming the cable car going down into the gorge below, and then he headed back to his car.

Jack arrived in Lithgow and went straight to the railway freight terminal and took out his fake Federal Police badge. He was really tired of wearing his brown wig and it was making his scalp itch, but he had no choice. People were looking for him and they were expecting him to be an ASIO agent, not a Federal officer. He considered himself to be in very dangerous territory because he was sure the back-hoe had been delivered here which meant that the friends of his enemies were here too. He needed to question these people about the delivery but just asking might set off alarm bells. Unfortunately there was no other way of asking about the back-hoe or the flat-bed carriage other than just asking and being ready to take evasive action if necessary.

'Hello dear, how can I help you?' asked the elderly woman at the front desk.

Jack flashed his badge and replied, 'I need to follow-up on a carriage which is currently parked in your terminal. It carried a cargo which we are interested in. Who can I speak to about that?'

'Andrew handles all our freight bookings, you can go ahead and see him in his office. Third door to your right.'

'Thank you,' said Jack and headed for Andrew's office. The nice thing about a small town like Lithgow was that the pace moved slow enough that you could speak to people without needing appointments.

He walked into Andrew's office and went through his routine of badge flashing followed by a question.

'Do you have the carriage number?' asked Andrew.

Jack read it to him from the note he had saved on his mobile phone.

Andrew bashed away on his keyboard for a few seconds then turned the computer monitor in Jack's direction so that he could see the results. Apparently Lithgow Coal Mining had taken delivery of whatever was on that carriage.

'Do you guys have security cameras covering the area were the cargo gets unloaded?' asked Jack. It had occurred to him that someone else may have taken the drums of radioactive material before the mining company fetched the delivery. Or perhaps the carriage had arrived without the drums of radioactive material. It could have been off loaded somewhere else along the way. He wanted to know what he was talking about before he went to the mining company and started asking awkward questions.

'I don't know for sure,' replied Andrew. 'I know we have security cameras out there but I don't know what they are pointed at. You should probably ask the security people.'

'Where can I find them?'

Andrew looked dumb founded for a moment then said, 'Actually I have never seen where they are based. I only have a phone number for them.' Andrew dialed a number and handed the receiver to Jack.

'Good afternoon sir,' said Jack. Security people were all about respect and self-importance. The more you gave the more they were willing to be helpful. 'I'm Federal Detective Brown and I would like to come over and view security footage of the railway terminal. It's related to an ongoing investigation.'

The security person gave Jack an office address in Lithgow where all the tapes were stored. Jack noted it down then thanked Andrew and left.

Jack walked into the office building at the address he was given. There had been no signage outside to identify the security occupants. Jack met a man in a security uniform and flashed his badge saying, 'Clive sent me. I need to view video surveillance from 2 October at the railway freight terminal.'

The security guard looked him up and down then said, 'Sure... this way.' He had not bothered to introduce himself or ask Jack's name and Jack had not offered it either. If you treated them on a professional *need to know* basis then they tended to respond likewise or risk looking stupid for not knowing security etiquette.

'Have a sit down... I'll bring the discs.'

Jack sat in front of a computer and then shortly after, he was given a stack of fourteen DVD discs.

'Is this all you got,' said Jack in mock sarcasm.

Security man smiled thinly and said, 'Our system only takes a picture every three seconds. We got fourteen cameras covering that train yard and we can fit twenty-four hours worth of data on a DVD disk. Just pop the disc in and watch at high-speed till you see what you are looking for.'

Jack placed the first disc in the computer DVD drive and it triggered an application to view the contents. He chose the high-speed option and the screen showed the train yard with trains and people moving in a rather comical fashion, similar to watching an old black-and-white movie but faster still. The recordings were also time coded in the bottom right corner. Some of the cameras where useless for his purposes and he could quickly set them aside without having to watch the entire days recording at high-speed.

Camera six looked promising, showing a side rail where carriages were shunted to after being detached from the main train. Jack watched and waited. It took about sixteen minutes to get through a twenty-four hour recording in this way. After about seven minutes he found it. A carriage containing a complete back-hoe was shunted to a side rail. More importantly, the camera clearly showed six large drums secured in the front bucket of the vehicle. *This was the one.*

Jack slowed the recording down a bit until he saw some people getting busy around the carriage. A one and a half ton truck had pulled up next to the carriage and then two men got out. The thinner of the two lowered its side flap while the big one got up on the carriage and began to tilt-roll a drum out the front bucket onto the back bed of the truck.

Jack recognized the build of the big man, it was the same as the man Renae had caught on camera when she filmed the train crash. He watched the jerky motion of the camera recording as it showed the two men unload the drums and drive off. The camera resolution was too poor to show the vehicle number plates or any valuable facial data of the two men, but Jack instinctively knew it was the man from the train crash. He continued watching and then sometime later another group of men arrived and unloaded the back-hoe from the carriage. They looked like mine employees and Jack saw some hard-hats on the dash-board of one of the vehicles they had arrived in. On the side of the vehicle was the wording *Consolidated Coal and Gas.*

Jack had what he wanted. He also wanted to pass this on to Randy via the secure server. If this computer was on a network which had internet access then he could do it from here but that might lead his enemies to his secure server. *Security man* had left Jack alone in the room with the computer so he had a bit of freedom to maneuver. The application which he was using to view the security footage had a feature whereby you could save sections of the footage to the computer hard drive. Jack marked off the section he wanted and saved it to a new file.

He opened Internet Explorer on the computer and up popped Google's search page. Excellent, he had internet access. Jack setup a new Gmail account and then created a new message and attached the portion of security footage he had isolated. Instead of sending the message, he saved it as a *draft*. He then deleted the browser history, closed it and finally deleted the file he had extracted from the security DVD. He returned the DVD's to *security man* and left

When he got back to his car, he accessed the Gmail account from his mobile phone and retrieved the uploaded file to his mobile phone before re-uploading it to his secure server and leaving a message for Randy. It was a bit of a run-around but it meant that if anyone in the security facility checked on his network activity, all they might find was the new Gmail account which had no traceable connection to his current whereabouts or his secure server address.

Jack checked his watch, it was 4:05 PM. He had just enough time to make it out to the coal mine. He assumed that the mine worked around the clock but the office admin staff would probably leave by 5:00pm.

Jack pulled up to the gate at the coal mine. It was one of many owned by *Consolidated Coal and Gas* according to a sign at the gate. He spoke to the gate security guard and was then directed to an office building to his left. He parked next to a Harley Davidson motorcycle and went inside.

A man in a hard-hat was busy at a nearby desk and looked up with a scowl when Jack approached.

'Hello, I'm Federal Detective Brown,' said Jack.

'So?' said hard hat.

'You having a bad day?' asked Jack.

'Something like that. Look we are kinda busy here. You got somin to say then spit it out.'

Jack assumed he was talking to the Harley owner. The man certainly looked the part with tattoos going up both arms and trying to live up to his idea of how bikers behaved. Jack could have taken him if he wanted to but the situation had not required it yet. He knew that under that hard outer façade was a person with a problem. He just had to find a way to connect. Had he known he would be dealing with an anti-police type of person then he may have chosen to use a different identity. Jack stayed calm and said, 'I parked next to your Harley. You've done a great job customizing it.'

'Stop kissing my ass cop, I don't swing that way. You gonna get to the point or am I going to have to toss yer ass outta here.'

Jack could have threatened him with obstructing justice but he tried being polite again. 'Look mate, it's clear to me that some cops must have pissed you off sometime in the past. Don't confuse me with them. I'm not here for you or your Harley. I'm looking for a back-hoe that some people from this mine picked up at the freight terminal three months ago.'

The man now seemed to look at Jack in a new light. He sized him up for a moment or two then seemed to decide to coöperate. 'Yeah I remember that. Some head office guy bought it from a mineral exploration company. It was in pretty good shape for used equipment. Why you interested?'

'We believe it was used in a crime, before you guys bought it,' said Jack. 'I just want to take a look at it and see if there's anything on it that can help us with our investigation.'

'Yeah okay,' said hard hat. 'It's busy laying pipe near our new western expansion. Carry on down this dirt road for about two kilometers and you should see it to you left.'

'Thank you,' said Jack and then he left. Hard hat guy watched him drive off, then he made a phone call.

The back-hoe was in a field near the side of the dirt road. A group of men were working around it, lowering a twelve-inch diameter pipe into a trench which the back-hoe was digging. Jack did not bother getting out of the car, he had already seen the external filter and compressor out of which ran a pipe to the cabin of the vehicle. It was a non-standard attachment and he knew it was meant to keep the cabin air breathable and slightly pressurized so that outside dust and particles would not penetrate into the cabin. The driver of this back-hoe was probably loving it but Jack knew that it would have been essential to have such a luxury when digging in radioactive dirt.

The men using it now were probably safe but he would alert Randy anyhow and get this vehicle properly decontaminated. Rain and wind would have cleaned off any remaining surface radioactive particles but it was possible that some of it remained deep in the tire treads and definitely in the air filter material, unless they had already replaced the filters during the last three months. He hoped that it was not the case. The air filter was located inside a protective housing and a police forensic team might still be able to find finger prints on it, finger prints belonging to whoever attached that equipment to the back-hoe.

Jack considered his next move. The back-hoe would need to be examined by a forensic team and hopefully that might generate new leads. It was also possible, but unlikely, that Randy would be able to extract useful information from the security footage from the railway freight terminal. For now, he had no new leads. He would have to wait to hear from Randy. It would be pointless to go back to Sydney because the radioactive drums where unloaded here in Lithgow. There had to be more clues here, perhaps someone saw something. He decided to head back to Lithgow and spend the night in a motel. Hopefully he would have some new ideas or leads in the morning.

Golakov hurried up the dirt path which led to the top of the hill. He had not had much time to prepare. His contact at the mine had phoned him about twenty minutes ago saying that a Federal Detective was there asking about the back-hoe. The contact was a biker he had intentionally befriended in a pub. Golakov had wanted a contact at the mine so that he would have inside information if anyone came snooping around. The gamble had paid off. Whoever this Fed was did not really matter, he was going to die.

At the top of the hill he found a spot with a good view of the road going to the mine. The Fed would be coming back this way. Golakov lay on the ground and looked through the scope on his VSS Vintorez sniper rifle.

He had barely done so when a four-wheel drive vehicle came into view with a driver matching the description of the Fed.

Chapter 9

Jack was driving back along the dirt road from the back-hoe. It was a bone jarring ride on a road built for convenience rather than comfort. The rock hard shock absorbers did little to ease the pain. Eventually he got onto a better road surface as he neared the mine office. The Harley was still parked there. Jack signed out at the gate and made his way down the mine access road which was at least tarred. The road had many bends in the hilly mine area but smoothed out a bit has it neared the main road from Lithgow.

He rounded another bend then suddenly something slammed through the engine cover and steam came hissing out. There was a small elongated round hole in the car about three feet in front of him and he realized that someone had taken a shot at him. He slammed on the brakes, weaving the vehicle from side to sided until it slowed enough for him to turn around.

Another bullet punched through the windscreen and spat glass onto his lap. It must have just missed his head by inches. He spun the car around and headed back the way he had come, weaving left and right as he drove.

The rear-view mirror suddenly exploded as a bullet ripped through it and just when Jack expected a bullet in the back, he rounded the bend and was temporarily safely out of sight of the shooter.

The first bullet must have damaged the water cooling system which meant that the engine would overheat and die in about ten minutes. Jack pulled over to the side of the road and popped the hood on the vehicle. He quickly examined the engine and saw that the bullet had punched a hole in the water reservoir. It was not as bad as he had initially thought. The hole was high enough so that enough water would remain in the vehicle to keep it cool… well for longer than ten minutes but not indefinitely. Jack shut the hood on the vehicle and got back behind the wheel.

His mind raced through a series of options. *Someone at the mine must have contacted the shooter and alerted them to his presence. He could not continue towards the main road because the shooter might still be waiting. He could not stay parked here because they might come looking and he would be a sitting duck. He could go back to the mine. He had seen other dirt roads joining this access road and there might be another way out of the area. There might be more shooters along the road … then again, probably not because they would have shot at him sooner. As a last resort he could abandon his vehicle and disappear into the thick bush on the side of the road.* He looked over at the bush but it was clearly not going to be a picnic in there. *Probably lots of snakes in there… Okay… drive!*

He started the engine and drove in the direction of the mine.

Golakov swore silently as the bullet ripped into the car. He had missed the driver. This was far from ideal conditions for a sniper shot. He had been rushed, breathing heavily from running up the side of the hill and had not had time to set his sights in for the distance. He had assumed that the Fed would have spent more time examining the back-hoe, looking for clues and evidence. Probably chase everyone out and declare it a fucking crime scene, but no, not this bloody Fed. He must have just looked at it and come straight back. *Fucking idiotic Fed!*

He squeezed off two more shots, one came really close but the bloody Fed was weaving across the road like a lunatic. He had spun the car around and was now weaving back in the direction he had come from. He would be out of sight around the bend in a few seconds. Golakov squeezed off two more shots. One shattered the rear-view mirror but the vehicle rounded the bend before he could fire more shots. Golakov stood up fuming. He wanted to smash his rifle into the ground but he stopped himself. It was a good rifle. He had seen the steam coming out of the vehicle and it would not last long before it broke down. He would have to chase after him and finish him off. As a precaution he had earlier told Todorova to park on the side of the main road to the east, in case the Fed went back that way.

Golakov started running back down the hill to where he had parked his utility vehicle.

He put the rifle on the floor on the passenger side and then gunned the engine into life. It was a 3L V6 Ford Falcon, very powerful and much-loved by tradesmen across Australia. He would catch that Fed in no time at all.

Jack was negotiating an inside bend where the road was hugging the mountain when out of the corner of his eye he saw a vehicle come round the outside bend he had just come through. It was going fast and it would catch up with him quickly. Jack tried going faster but his top-heavy four-wheel drive was not built for high-speed cornering. It leaned and lurched through each bend and changed direction on every bump.

Jack fought hard but in less than a minute the other vehicle had caught up with him. He looked in his only remaining side mirror and recognized the burly shoulders and thick neck and head of the other driver as belonging to the man who had rolled the toxic drums off the carriage at the railway freight terminal.

The man was looking at him with hatred and contempt... then he rammed his vehicle into the back of Jack's 4WD making it lurch towards the edge of the road. Jack pulled the vehicle back towards the road and it leaned so far over that it must have ridden on only two wheels. He straightened it out as the road curved the other way and the two airborne wheels slammed back onto the road surface again, causing the vehicle to pull sharply to the left. Jack pulled it back to the right but the top of the vehicle scrapped against the rock wall on his left and then both side windows shattered in a shower of glass.

Jack looked in his mirror again. The driver behind him was now grinning an evil grin. He knew he had him and he was starting to enjoy his little death game. Jack thought hard. His vehicle was no match for the other... on tar, but if he went off-road he would have the advantage. He had to get onto one of those side roads he had seen.

Just then his vehicle got hit from behind again. Once again it lurched across the road but Jack could not pull it all the way back this time. The two right hand side wheels started to go off the edge of the road. Jack glanced down the embankment next to him. It was quite steep, perhaps

45 degrees but it flattened out near the bottom as it melded into another road, a dirt road.

If he just let the vehicle slide sideways off the road it would roll down the embankment and break apart on the dirt road below. He would probably be killed or badly injured, perhaps tossed out of the vehicle as it rolled. However, if he got the nose of the vehicle pointing down the embankment then it might stay on its wheels and it might be a more survivable situation. Jack spun the wheel hard to the right.

The heavy 4WD vehicle left the road and then time seemed to slow down dramatically for Jack. He watched as in slow motion the vehicle flew into the air, the land dropping away beneath it. Then the vehicle slowly began to drop as well and the land below came closer. The vehicle began to tilt with the nose dropping while the embankment came ever closer.

When they met, the embankment and the vehicle were at nearly the same angle but the vehicle still had momentum from the direction it was going before it left the road. It kicked up dirt, small rocks and bushes as it expended that momentum against all that got in its way and then it knew only one direction, down.

The vehicle was now heading straight down the side of the embankment and nearing the bottom, going fast. Jack starting steering it ever so slightly to the right, risking a roll but he had to now get the vehicle to go down the dirt road, not across it where it would plough into thick bushes and then more rocks.

Just as it hit bottom, the vehicle was still not quite pointed sufficiently enough down the road and it went across and started kicking up the thick bushes on the left of the road, flattening several of them and slowing him down just enough so that he could finally wrench the vehicle fully back onto the dirt road. He had made it. He had no clue where he was going but at least he was still in one piece.

Golakov laughed out loud as the Fed's car went off the road. He had survived the first impact but the car had taken damage. The stupid Fed had been lucky that time, had his car not managed to find its way back onto the road, he would be dead. But it was okay, he was enjoying knocking the Fed's car around and then watching him try to recover.

He could do that all day but he had work to do so he had hit him again, harder. The Fed's car had headed to the edge of the road and it looked like he was going to keep it from going over but then at the last moment the bloody idiot had actually turned off the road. It was unbelievable that someone could be so stupid but he had just witnessed it.

He slammed on the brakes and parked on the left of the road. Golakov wanted to take a picture of the Fed's crumpled car so he took his camera out from the glove compartment and walked to the edge of the road. At first he only saw a dust trail all the way to the bottom of the hill but then as he watched, the dust cloud at the bottom of the hill started moving down a dirt road. Golakov could not believe it. The Fed was so lucky that he had somehow managed to survive going off the side of the mountain and land on a road but even more unbelievable was the fact that his car was still going. That was one tough car, he had to get himself one of those.

He now had to chase after him again and kill him properly this time. The dirt road behind the Fed seemed to double back on itself and then it joined the tarred mine access road about two hundred meters from where he now stood. Golakov walked back to his car. The Fed had gained a short head start but he had the faster car and would catch him again quickly.

He started his car again and revved it a few times, enjoying the throaty roar of the engine, then he sped off, throwing up a shower of grit behind him before his fast accelerating tires met with the tar road and screamed a black streak onto its surface.

A few seconds later he did a sideways rally style entrance onto the dirt road on which the Fed was now traveling. He drove down through the switchback, kicking up another shower of grit as he did another sideways slide through the corner then he straightened out onto the long straight section where the Fed's car had landed. Up ahead was a dust cloud marking the spot where the Fed's car now was. It was not far, he would be there in under twenty seconds.

Jack drove as fast as he dared go in his unwieldy vehicle. The sun was very low and it was hard to see where he was going. His front left head light was smashed from the impact with the rock wall earlier and his right hand side lamp was pointing off into the bushes on his left, making night driving that much harder. He knew that his attacker would realize that he had survived and would probably try again. They might try shooting again but the bumpy dirt road and the dust cloud behind him would make for a difficult target. His attacker would most likely choose to chase him down and try to force him off the road again.

He glanced in his mirror but it was not there anymore. That last encounter with the bushes at the bottom of the hill had taken it. He shot a quick glance behind him but the dust cloud he was kicking up obscured his visibility in that direction. He would have little to no warning of another vehicle attack. His heavy vehicle had a slight advantage here because his attackers light vehicle was rear wheel driven and it was a utility vehicle which meant it did not have much weight and traction at the back.

It would be much harder to force him off the road now.

Suddenly Jack sensed or perhaps heard a change in the road noise. Another vehicle was close behind him. He shot another look over his shoulder and confirmed what he had heard. His attacker had caught up with him again. Ahead of Jack was another bend to the right. A smart advanced driver would try to get between him and the inside of the bend, forcing him outside and then off the road. Jack steered over to his right. He was taking a huge gamble because here in Australian people drive on the left which meant he was approaching a blind corner on the wrong side of the road. If a mining truck was coming up the hill around that corner he would smash straight into it but he had to take the chance.

Jack looked over his left shoulder, half expecting to see the vehicle come round that side now but his attacker was still behind him. Jack was going to have to slow down for the corner and his attacker was not going to let him do that. Jack steered slightly to the left but not so much as to leave a car sized gap on his right. His attacker followed. Jack took his opportunity. He jerked his vehicle back to the right hand side of the road and slammed on the brakes. The right side of the vehicle behind him ploughed into him and its light rear section started sliding out to the left. His attacker now had no choice but to also brake and correct his slide which allowed Jack the chance to make it around the bend. Looking over his left shoulder he saw his attackers vehicle right behind his, going around the corner sideways kicking out dirt as it did so. *He's a damn good driver*, thought Jack.

At the bottom of the hill ahead of Jack was a lake, obviously man-made and part of the mine processing plant. As he approached, the land flattened out and the road widened considerably, leaving him nowhere to hide. His attacker moved up alongside him and then just when he was about to swing hard into him, Jack anticipated the move and swung hard to the left. His heavy vehicle slammed the other one away quite harshly. The driver tried to recover but his vehicle hit a small bump and became airborne, only about two feet off the ground, but it meant that the driver had zero control, he was now just a passenger until his wheels met solid ground and found new traction. A second or two later the vehicle touched down again but it was now faced sideways to its direction of travel. The driver floored the accelerator to get traction and turn the vehicle but it was too late. It went over the side of the lake embankment and hit the water with an almighty splash.

Jack slammed on the brakes and slid to a halt. His dust cloud overtook him and continued going like a carriage without a horse. He stayed in the car, waiting for the dust to clear. It was getting darker but there was just enough light reaching the lake from the processing plant for him to make out the other vehicle's roof just barely breaching the surface. It stayed there for a few seconds then sank among a flotilla of bubbles.

A few men from the plant came walking over to see what had happened so Jack got out and showed them his fake

Federal badge, telling them it was all under control and that backup was on the way. He did not want any of them calling the police just yet. He walked closer to the water's edge trying to see if anyone had made it out alive. He needed to question the driver but he was not going to risk swimming out into a dark lake and confront and elephant sized man by himself. Hopefully the police would extract the vehicle and use its registration details to try to trace the driver. Randy would then be able to tap into the police report and give him the data he needed. Jack was desperate to update the secure server with the latest data he had but had not had a chance to do so yet. He was having quite a day. Turning to one of the men he asked, 'What's the quickest route back to the main road?'

'Just carry on past the plant, the road rejoins the R40 just before Bell.' Jack recalled that Bell was a small town not to far outside Lithgow.

'Thanks,' said Jack, then added. 'The driver of that vehicle is very dangerous. If he did survive you should not approach him… He might also be carrying a weapon.'

The miners now seemed more cautious. They had not reacted to Jack's warning until he mentioned the possible weapon. It seems they were quite willing to take on the driver but not so brave at the thought of him having a weapon.

'I need to go track down his accomplice now,' said Jack to the men. In reality he just wanted to get the hell out of there before police got wind of the situation and set up road blocks. He walked over to his car and man-handled the working headlight so that it pointed in front of the vehicle again, then he got in his car and left.

Golakov swam under water, away from the lights of the processing plant, clutching his rifle and camera. He had grabbed them as he swam out the passenger side window of his car. When he could no longer hold his breath he surfaced with his face up and took in air without sticking his whole head out the water. Fed's usually had guns and sticking you head out of the water was sure to get it blown off.

He sank back under the water and continued swimming to the far side of the lake and then carefully lifted his head halfway out the water so the he could look back with one exposed eye. The Fed was standing on the water edge, looking for him.

Golakov tried crawling out onto the embankment but his hand slipped on the mud and his heavy body pushed his rifle and camera deep into the soft mud. He looked back to the other side of the lake but they had not heard the small splash he had made. Machinery at the processing plant had drowned out any noise he had made. The Fed turned and walked back to a group of men who were gathering there, probably trying to organize a search party.

His rifle was now useless with mud having penetrated the working mechanism and the telescopic sights were probably out of alignment assuming that they still worked. Trying to fire it now would be lethal. The bullet would jam in the barrel and blow the rifle apart. Golakov left it in the mud and carefully covered it up to avoid detection.

With both hands now free, he managed to crawl out the water and up the embankment, nearly slipping once or twice. He got to the top just in time to see the Fed driving away. Most of the men were returning to their posts at the plant but two of them hung around talking and pointing at where his vehicle had disappeared into the water. The Fed had probably called for police backup but was not waiting for them.

Typical Feds, thought Golakov. They always thought they were above and better than the local police. He had worked as a Bulgarian police officer for several years after he left school and had met many such know it all Federal police. Eventually he had hit one, breaking his jaw and almost his neck. A judge had given him a choice of going to jail or joining the army. He chose the military and they had taught him all his special skills and shown him respect. But he still hated *special* police.

He reached into his pocket and took out his mobile phone but it was dead, probably water damaged, so he tossed back into the lake and started walking. He needed to call Todorova and alert him that the Fed was heading his way.

He headed around the lake to the processing plant, to where a few vehicles were parked outside a tall corrugated metal building. The two men who had stayed behind at the lake side were now walking slowly back to the processing plant, talking as they went, their backs towards him.

Golakov walked fast, putting his weight on the outer edges of his feet to reduce the sound of his foot falls. Once again the machinery from the processing plant was louder than any sounds he was making.

He neared the two men then grabbed them by the neck and bashed their heads together, face first. Their teeth broke against each other and cut through lips and tongue. Both now also had broken noses and were in too much pain and shock to react in time to ward off his second attack. He pulled them apart to his full arm length and then bashed their faces together a second time, his powerful pectoral muscles bulging and going rock had with the effort. He heard a bone crunching sound as their skulls cracked and neck vertebrae separated and then he let them drop to the ground where he frisked them and removed a mobile phone and car keys from one of them.

He left the bodies lying there and walked towards the parked cars, dialing Todorova's number, then speaking to him briefly in Slavic.

###

Jack was approaching Chafney road, also called the R40, which was one of two east bound roads going out of Lithgow. The other road was the infamous Great Western Highway which was nine kilometers south of his present location. If any mine workers had alerted the police, they would be coming from Lithgow along Chafney road. His damaged vehicle with one head lamp was sure to draw police attention so his best chance of avoiding them was to drive to Bell then take the connecting road south to the Great Western Highway.

He turned left onto Chafney road then three kilometers later he entered the small town of Bell then took the right fork onto the Darling Causway which would take him south. Bell was so small it did not even have a traffic light. He had briefly seen two houses to his left and that was it. Jack drove on wondering what the heck Bell was all about. *Did two houses really constitute a town?* he wondered. There had been some traffic on Chafney road but this south bound road was really quiet. Jack glanced over his shoulder to look for traffic behind him and saw only one set of head lights, moving at a normal pace. No one was chasing him it seemed.

Todorova was waiting on Chafney road at the point where the tarred mine access road joined it. The plan was to act as a back door in the unlikely event that the Fed (Jack) survived Golakov's rifle shots and continued on past him. Todorova was to block the road and finish him off.

He waited for about twenty minutes then his phone rang. He did not recognize the number of the caller so he answered it and did not speak. It was Golakov telling him that the Fed had escaped and was heading down a dirt road which would meet up with Chafney road near Bell.

Todorova hung up the phone and started his engine. Bell was about five kilometers ahead of him and there was a good chance that the Fed would get there before him. If he was returning to Lithgow then he would drive right past Todorova. Golakov had told him that the Fed's car only had one working headlight, making it rather easy to spot at night. No such vehicle had passed him yet.

He waited for a gap in the traffic then pulled out onto Chafney road and headed towards Bell. The road was busy enough to prevent him from exceeding the speed limit and he had no choice but to follow along like everyone else.

A while later he reached the spot where the dirt road joined Chafney road. The Fed had not passed him so he must have either pulled over on the dirt road or had gone the other way towards Bell. If the Fed had pulled over on the dirt road, Golakov would find him.

Todorova continued driving towards Bell and then reached the fork in the road where the southern connecting road joined Chafney road. *Now what?* thought Todorova. The Fed had either continued on towards Sydney or he had forked onto the connecting road which would take him to the Great Western Highway. Todorova made his choice and took the connecting road. He figured that if the Fed had continued on to Sydney it would be very difficult to catch up with him and there would be too many witnesses if he tried to run him off the road. This connecting road was quiet, so if the Fed had come this way he could catch up with him and run him off the road then kill him. Tomorrow night was their big night and they were no longer pussy footing around. They could not afford to be stopped this late in the game.

Up ahead at a distance he saw some tail lights. Todorova accelerated a bit to catch up but not so much that it would alert the other driver. As he drew near he realized that this car had two head lights, it was not the Fed. He overtook the vehicle and continued.

In the distance he saw more tail lights and when he had caught up he could see that something was different with this cars lights. It was difficult to tell for sure when viewing the car from behind. It was a 4WD but was it the right one? Todorova followed for a while then when the vehicles was going around a left hand curve he became convinced that it did not have a front left head lamp. The road immediately in front of the left side of the vehicle was dark whereas the other side was light.

A sign next to the road read *Mount Victoria, 3 KM.* Todorova decided to act now, before the Fed got to the next town. He moved forward and began to overtake at a comfortable pace like a regular driver might do. Just as he came next to the Fed he spun the wheel hard to his left, crashing his car into the other. The Fed's car veered left and he was quick to react, spinning his steering wheel to the right but suddenly something collapsed and he saw the front left side of the Fed's car drop, then it veered left again and left the road, going down an embankment towards the train lines. It must have hit the train lines hard because Todorova saw the headlight suddenly pointing skywards at a crazy angle then it went sideways and rolled through the bushes on the other side of the train lines.

Jack was nearing Mount Victoria when a vehicle began overtaking him, He was sticking with the speed limit so as not to draw attention and he no longer trusted his vehicle to the pointed where he was going to drive it fast. It had endured quite a beating and he needed to get rid of it before it broke down completely. The vehicle overtaking him appeared to behaving normally but as a precaution, Jack gripped the steering wheel hard and prepared for a possible vehicle attack.

It happened suddenly and Jack corrected in time and would have made it but the front left steering rod and suspension broke. The front left wheel then, of its own accord, turned hard left and the vehicle veered left again.

Jack knew he now had no control, he could either ride it out and take his chances or jump out. He shot a glance ahead of him to see what his likely fate was going to be. The vehicle appeared to be going down a steep embankment headed for a double train line. It might tip and roll at any second...

He unclipped his seat belt, flung open his door and dove out into the blackness next to him. He landed in thick brush and long grass and grabbed handfuls of it in an attempt to slow himself as he slid down the embankment. He came to rest at the bottom, just meters from the stoney ballast supporting the nearest train line. He had also seen his car crash into the same stony ballast just seconds before he got there. The front had dug in, flipping the car over as it cleared both railway lines before crash landing on the other side and rolling several times before finally coming to a halt in thick bush.

Jack had twisted his ankle badly and he felt like he had been run over by a train. He glanced back up the steep embankment he had just slid down. His attacker would most likely come looking to make sure he was dead and kill him if he was not. He had to keep low and get the hell away from there.

He crawled south along the edge of the embankment and after about thirty meters he noticed that the embankment was now angled less steeply and then after another few meters he found a path coming down from the road above. *Oh crap*, though Jack. Would his attacker have seen the path and be making his way down it this very instant.

He looked up the embankment and saw... nothing. He looked back the way he had come and saw torch-light. Someone was searching the bottom of the embankment where his car had hit the train line. There was enough reflected torch-light for Jack to see that the person was holding both arms out in front of them, one crossed over the other about halfway along the forearm. It was the stance used by military trained people when holding both a torch and a weapon.

The person was assuming that Jack may have been ejected out of the vehicle when it hit the bottom. He would probably search an area along the trail left by the vehicle as it rolled into the bush. When he reached the vehicle he would find it empty and realize that Jack was alive which would encourage him to look even harder. He may even have called his mates. Perhaps more gunmen where on their way there right now.

Jack crawled, ran and hopped his way up the path to the road on top. He recognized his attackers car parked on the side of the road about ten meters from the path Jack had come up. The attacker had not seen the path but had instead walked back up the road to where Jack had gone off the edge and then made his way down the steep embankment, searching as he went. Jack looked down towards the railway line and saw that the torch-bearer was now searching the ground between the train lines and Jack car. In about a minute he would realize that the car was empty.

Jack limped along to his attackers car. He wanted to search it for any clues about who these people were and from where they were operating. Their base had to be nearby because they could never haven gotten to him so quickly if they were based in Sydney. He had to act quickly. Jack carefully tried the driver side door, it was open. Better yet, the keys were in the ignition. The driver had been too focused on Jack to bother with taking the keys with him. Another idea occurred to Jack, *forget searching, take the whole damn car!*

He yanked the door all the way open and the car interior light cam on. He had expected that and quickly reached up and put it off, but it was too late. The rear side window shattered as a bullet flew through it and exited through the roof. His attacker had seen him. Jack crouched low and turned the ignition. The engine started first time. He slipped the car into gear and took off. This was his best lead yet and he felt elated despite the pain in his bruised body.

Chapter 10

Jack drove along the Great Western Highway towards Lithgow, staying alert to the possibility of new attacks.

He wanted to get the car off the road to a safe place where he could search it properly but had not seen any suitable locations. He decided he may as well try the back streets of Lithgow. A school or a church would be empty at this time of night and he might be able to find an out of sight place to park on their property. Schools were often gated and locked whereas church properties were usually open to welcome their flock. The risk was that driving a car round the back of a church at night would be guaranteed to arouse suspicion from anyone who may have seen or heard the activity. He decided to make that a last resort and to keep an eye out for other options.

As Jack entered Lithgow he spotted a video store. It was closed but he noticed a side alley next to it which presumably led to a small parking section at the rear where the staff would park. He turned and drove down the alleyway and as expected found a small six car parking area at the back, fully enclosed by a six-foot wall.

He parked the car and began looking through the interior. The glove box held some registration papers for the vehicle. He took some pictures of it with his mobile phone. There was nothing else of interest inside but a forensic team might find useful DNA and finger prints, perhaps some hair. Jack tried to reduce his own finger prints as much as possible and then wiped the steering wheel and gear knob plus the door handles where he had touched. Leaving his finger prints here would just help strengthen the patsy case against him so he hoped the vehicle owner had left enough prints on other areas of the car for police to find.

Next Jack removed the car keys and opened the trunk. There were three large plastic buckets labeled *strontium carbonate*, *barium chloride* and *calcium chloride* . Jack waved his wristwatch past the buckets but got no radioactive reading. He took some pictures of the plastic buckets but found nothing else of interest in the trunk. He was about to drop the keys in the trunk and shut it so that it would be found when the police broke into the trunk, but decided against it. He would rather take the keys with him because one of them might open something important.

So where to next? thought Jack. He was tired and would love to soak in a bath but hotels were out of the question. A late night hotel check-in would be easily found by an enemy, especially in a small town like Lithgow which probably had no more than five or six hotels. He could not sleep in the car because his enemies might find it here and he would be a sitting, sleeping, soon to be dead duck.

He walked over to the nearest six-foot wall and pulled himself up high enough to see over the top. It was a residential property with a nice garden and some trees.

One of the trees had what appeared to be a rope ladder hanging from it. Jack followed the ladder up with his eyes and saw a box like construction at the top of it... a tree house and it was a good enough place to spend the night.

He scanned the garden looking for a kennel. He did not want to deal with a barking dog or something more ferocious. It seemed clear, but it was dark and he could not be certain. *Surely a dog would have barked when he had parked the car?* He just had to take the chance.

Jack scaled the wall and slid silently down the other side, bending both knees as he landed to absorb the impact and sound. He waited and listened before moving, ready to jump back over the wall if a dog came out of the dark. Nothing happened so he quietly made his way to the tree house and gently tested the robe ladder. It seemed sturdy enough so he climbed up and stopped at the top to use his mobile phone display as a small light, shining it on the floor of the tree house. As he rule he never assumed that floors were automatically safe to walk on just because they existed. People dumped all kinds of crap in spaces they were not using and tree houses were no exception. This one however was clean and even had some sort of carpet on its floor. *Lucky kids,* thought Jack. He pulled himself up into the tree house and lay on his side while he typed a message to Randy via the secure server. He also uploaded the pictures he had taken of the car and the chemicals in the trunk then he rested his head on his arm and he fell into a light sleep.

Randy was lying sleeping on his back in bed, his iPod and headphones lying on the floor next to him. He had earlier been listening to Katie Melua because he felt that her soothing voice helped to calm him and melt the day's stress away. His phone suddenly starting sounding an alarm and when Randy woke and peered at the screen through dreary eyes he saw a black and yellow radiation symbol. He had set up a system to alert him whenever Jack updated the secure server with new intel and he had thought that the radiation symbol was cool, given what they were dealing with.

Randy read Jack's update and sat up wide awake when he read how someone had first tried to shoot Jack then run him off the road, twice. Jack had managed to steal one of the vehicles and hide it. The trunk of that vehicle had contained some strange chemicals. Randy followed Jack's instructions and logged a request with the police forensic department in Sydney asking that they go retrieve the vehicle in the lake and the one behind the video store and do a forensic examination. He advised them to treat it as high priority because it was related to National Security and possibly involved a bomb. This meant that they had to do it **now,** not the following day.

Randy then looked at the list of chemicals and memorized them. He would have to do an ASIO database search the following morning and find out what those chemicals were typically used for and then cross reference that list against companies in the Lithgow area who were likely to be doing the type of work which involved the use of those chemicals. He could not do anything about it now though.

He logged a reply to Jack on the secure server and advised him that police forensics would be fetching the vehicles and that he would investigate the chemicals first thing in the morning.

Jack woke up to the sound of people talking and a car door closing. He checked his watch and saw that it was just after 5:00 AM. The sky was also just starting to get light in the east. He edged towards the door of his tree house and peeped out. The height of his tree house allowed him to see over the top of the six-foot wall and he could see several policemen and some forensic people who were busy examining the vehicle he had left behind the video store.

He had to get out of there soon before the owners of the house woke up and started their day. If he climbed out of the tree house now, he would be visible to any of the police who happened to look up in his direction. He would have to time it carefully. Jack decided to first check for messages from Randy so he logged into the secure server. He found an update from Randy saying that he had organized the retrieval of the two vehicles and would run a database search and cross-reference on the chemicals this morning. Jack realized that he would have to wait about three hours before he would get more news from Randy. That was more than enough time to go get cleaned up, eat some breakfast and rent another car. He would just have to pick a different car rental company considering what had happened to his previous car.

The police were still busy next door so Jack carefully kept watch, waiting for an opportunity to get out of the tree house. Eventually the police seemed to be getting ready to leave. They had moved the vehicle out of the tiny parking area and positioned it at the end of the side alley where Jack could just see the rear portion of a tow truck which was busy attaching its lifting apparatus to the vehicle. The forensic team had also covered the vehicle in something resembling a tarpaulin, probably to try to preserve any external evidence on the vehicle. They began winching the vehicle onto the back of the tow truck and then Jack took his chance and quickly climbed down from the tree house. The fence around the residential property was a four-foot wooden paling fence so Jack did an easy two-handed vault maneuver and swung his legs over, landing quietly on the other side.

He now found himself on a road which ran parallel to the main street going through Lithgow. He had no idea where it went so he decided to follow it for two blocks then rejoin the main street and look for somewhere to eat.

It was a bit of a chilly morning as well, Lithgow was situated fairly high up in the Blue Mountains and on average had temperatures running ten degrees cooler than Sydney. Jack estimated the current temperature to be around 18° C and the brisk walk he was doing was a welcome warm up. A woman with a big German Sheppard dog was approaching Jack, out on her morning walk.

'G'day,' she said.

Jack smiled and noticed that the dog was also friendly, giving a slight wag of its tail, so he stopped and said, 'Hello, what a beautiful dog you have.' He patted the dog's head and gave a few scratches behind its ear. It was not an act, he actually liked dogs but he needed to find out where a mall or a Mac Donald's was so that he could get breakfast.

'Her name is Shelly,' said the woman looking pleased and trusting Jack.

'Hello Shelly,' said Jack and bent down to make a fuss of the dog who barked and wagged her tail furiously. Jack stood up again, made as if to continue walking then turned and asked, 'Do you know of a good place to buy breakfast, I'm visiting with friends and I want to take them out for a treat.'

'Oh sure. There's a Mac Donald's just about a kilometer up the road,' she said pointing north, 'and about a block before that, if you turn right you'll see the mall. They have a food court and a few restaurants.'

'That's good to know, thank you,' said Jack and then continued his brisk walk, heading north.

The food court in the mall was mostly deserted, it was still too early, so Jack went to the public toilets and did his best to freshen up. He had intentionally left his brown wig in the tree house. It was filthy from when he had jumped out of his car and slid down the embankment, plus it was no longer useful as a disguise. The men who tried to kill him yesterday would be looking for a light brown-haired male. He carried a wallet with money and fake ID's in his pocket but his small suitcase with clothes was still in the trunk of his rental car which now lay smashed among bushes at Mount Victoria. He decided to buy a new shirt when the shops opened.

At 7:00 AM he found a restaurant in the mall which had just opened so he ordered an English Breakfast and coffee. He checked the secure server again while he waited and found a new update from Randy. The car Jack had stolen had in turn been stolen from someone in Cairns about four months back. The current registration papers which Jack had photographed we fake, or more precisely, they belonged to a real person in Sydney but it was a case of identity theft. Another dead-end.

Jack parked his new rental car in the parking lot behind the Lithgow mall. It was another big heavy four-wheel drive, just in case he had to go off-road again. This one was still quite new and even smelt new. Hopefully nothing bad would happen to it.

Randy had updated the secure server with a list of companies in the area who, to a greater or lesser degree, used the chemicals he had found in the trunk of the car he stole. At the top of the list, the only company which used all three of the chemicals, was a fireworks factory in Wallerwang called Cooper and Sons.

Jack decided he would have to go pay them a visit. It was very likely that the person he was looking for was an employee there or perhaps he was a supplier or a representative from a supplier. There were many possibilities and the only way to narrow it down further was to go there and talk to some people at that company.

He also had to be careful, his enemies might anticipate his move and be waiting to take another shot at him.

The road to the factory had been quite uneventful and pleasant. The factory was situated twelve kilometers north-west of Lithgow on a few acres of farmland surrounded by pine trees. It also had a good view of Lake Wallace which was about one kilometer distant. Based on the size of the place, Jack estimated that they employed around eighty people. Today, being 31 December, it was mostly deserted but they did have a security guard at the gate. Jack stopped in front of the gate and the guard came to his window.

'We are closed today sir,' said the guard.

Jack took out a fake ID for a police detective and said, 'I'm detective Morris. We have a situation regarding contamination with some of your products. Is there anyone on site who can answer a few questions for me and show me around?'

'Mr Franklin is here loading some equipment for the Sydney event tonight. I'll call him on his mobile.'

'Tell me where he is and I'll go find him,' said Jack.

'Sorry, can't do that. Somebody has to accompany you.'

Jack protested, 'I'm a policeman, I'm not going to steal anything.'

'Does not matter sir, you could be the president and I still wont let you in,' said the guard firmly. He dialed a number on his mobile phone and spoke to the other party for a few seconds, then walked to the gate and opened it. He motioned to Jack to drive and stop in front of him. Jack did so and the guard came back to his window and said, 'Park you vehicle on the left of the gate in the visitors parking area and wait for Mr Franklin. He will be with you shortly.' The guard watched Jack intently as he drove in and parked his vehicle and it was obvious to Jack that he was expected to do nothing else but wait or risk the wrath of the security guard. Jack decided that he liked the security guard. Anyone coming in here would get the message that this was not a place to mess around in. Take it seriously or stay out.

About three minutes later another man came walking around the corner of the building and headed for Jack's car. He seemed friendlier but also carried an air of responsibility with him. Jack got out the car to introduced himself again.

'Mr Franklin?' asked Jack.

'Yes, you can call me Bill...'

Jack showed his ID and said, 'Detective Andrew Morris. Andrew will do. Yesterday some of our people intercepted a vehicle carrying chemicals which, we understand, are used at this factory. That vehicle had been used in a crime so we just need to get some information from you guys about how those chemicals are used.'

'What were the chemicals?' asked Bill.

'Strontium carbonate, barium chloride and calcium chloride', said Jack.

'Oh, yeah those gets added to our fireworks to produce various colors. We don't use it in some type of chemical process, it just gets thrown in as is and when it gets ignited in the final stage explosion of a rocket or mortar, then it produces a shower of sparkles in a color specific to the chemical mixture used.'

Jack thought this over for a moment then felt the blood drain from his face and a chill went through him as he realized the magnitude of the problem.

'Is something wrong?' asked Bill upon seeing the change in Jack's composure.

'Something could be very wrong,' said Jack. 'Where do you store your fireworks?'

'We have very little on site at the moment. Our last production push has just recently ended and the product has been shipped out to the new years events in Sydney and Perth. Sydney is especially big this year, we got Prince William and Kate putting in an appearance at the Opera House and it's going to be big, millions of people expected.'

Jack was still trying to figure out how his enemies had managed to tie themselves to this event. He still had no real evidence and he did not want to tell Bill what his real suspicions were. He tried another approach. 'Can you show me where you packed the chemicals into the fireworks then?'

'Yes, I can do that,' said Bill. He could see that Jack was holding back on something important. 'Let's go round this way.'

They walked around the small admin building by the visitors parking and then Bill unlocked the door into the assembly section. He pointed out a long bench with various bits of equipment along the way.

'We pack the explosives in a different section because... well you know, it's dangerous and we want to minimize the risk to our people. The payload as we call it, gets packed here. The chemical powder mix gets compressed into cylinders in this machine, the size of the die would depend on what launch vehicle is being used. Rockets are generally of a much smaller diameter than mortars.'

Jack held his wristwatch next to the metal die used to compress the chemicals and just as he was about to pull his hand back, it started to beep.

'What's that for?' asked Bill.

'The chemical mixture you used has been contaminated,' said Jack, intentionally leaving out the word *radioactive*. He did not want to panic Bill just yet, it would be smarter to first gather some more data and formulate a plan of action.

'With what?' said Bill defensively. 'We use well-known suppliers ...' His voice trailed off.

'Did you think of something?' asked Jack.

'The theme for this year's event in Sydney is going to be mainly purple. It was a late change of plan. Usually we prepare months in advance for an event. Sydney's event products were already done and dusted when we heard that there was going to be royalty in attendance and the Mayor requested that we do a purple theme to honor them. It meant we had to pull the payload off about fifty percent of the product and repack it with a purple mix. Fortunately someone found a supplier who had some premixed purple product and we bought that to get it done in time.'

Jack took his phone out of his pocket and called up the picture of the car he had stolen. He moved to stand next to Bill and show him the picture but at that instant the phone exploded out of his hand and Bill sank to the ground with blood pumping out of a hole where his heart used to be.

Chapter 11

Jack fell to the ground and started leopard crawling towards the door. There was nothing he could do for Bill.

The bullet had come through a window to his right and there were only pine trees in that direction. Whoever had shot Bill was hiding among those trees and would spot Jack long before he had a chance to see them. He did not know for sure if the bullet was intended for him or Bill. Probably both.

He lay on the floor trying to formulate a plan. He had to get back to Sydney and somehow stop those fireworks from going off. The Harbor Bridge, the Opera House, the ferry terminal at Circular Quay, thirty or so restaurants and millions of people watching the fireworks were going to have radioactive dust blown all over them when those purple fireworks exploded. Prince William and his bride would be among the casualties who were destined to die a painful and slow death from radioactive poisoning. The whole area would be a no-go zone for a very long time while people did their best to decontaminate it.

Jack checked his watch. It was 11:00 AM. The first of the fireworks usually went off at 8:00 PM which gave him nine hours to somehow prevent a disaster. Then suddenly he heard the sound of footsteps outside. They stopped outside the door and Jack frantically looked around him for cover. He had no idea if it was friend or foe at the door and besides, the obvious assumption would be that Jack had shot Bill. After all, he was a fugitive bomb maker according to the *real* police. The building he was in had another entrance on the far side. To get there he would have to sprint down the length of the building, exposing himself to the row of windows from where the bullet had come. Alternatively, if he had time, he could crawl the distance keeping below the lower end of the windows to avoid detection.

The door began to open to the outside and Jack recognized the uniform of the gate security guard, then suddenly the guards chest exploded in a spray of red mist and chunks of flesh, followed by the harsh bark of a shotgun. The sound had been really close, maybe ten meters away. There were *two* shooters here now.

Jack got to his feet and sprinted to the far side door. There was no time to waste. Glass exploded to his right as another bullet tore through a window. He leaped over Bills body and continued going. Reaching the far side, he did a baseball slide and went feet first into the door. Staying low, he lifted his hand up to the door handle and tried to open it. It was locked. *Now what!*

Once again Jack did a quick study of his surroundings. The windows were the type which consisted of many smaller panels in a metal frame. The individual panes were too small to allow him to run and jump through them. They might open somehow but he would not have the time to stand there and figure it out. He would be dead before he got out that way. Then he noticed a trap door in the floor at the end of the long workbench. Did it go somewhere? The shotgun shooter was busy dragging the security guards body out the way. He had tried to open the door but the body had prevented it. In a second or two he would be inside and coming for him.

Jack crawled over to the trap door and pulled it up. It was of stud metal construction and it opened to the right, blocking the window shooters view of Jack. He peered down the hole and saw a metal chute going at an angle towards the rear of the building. It was big enough for him to fit through. Jack lowered his body into the chute and let go just as the window shooter fired a round which hit the trap door and knocked it back down.

The chute took Jack to a paved area behind the building and expunged him about two meters up in the air. Jack curved his legs and twisted cat-like to get his feet under him as he landed then rolled once and took off running again towards the next building where he stopped behind its north side, placing it between him and the shooter in the pine trees. To the west where he had come in he noticed thick black smoke rising up into the air. The admin building was on fire, probably set alight by Mr Shotgun. Beyond that was his car but it was very likely that they had sabotaged it to trap him in here. That smoke would attract people's attention and bring police and fire engines, but they had to come all the way from Lithgow. His attackers obviously knew that they had about twenty minutes to clean up this place before it got to hot to handle.

Just then a huge hole exploded through the wooden door at the back of the building he had just come out of. Then someone kicked it fully open and Jack recognized the big guy whose car he had knocked into the lake yesterday. He was alive... and laughing at Jack as he cocked another round into the breach of the shotgun.

Behind the shotgun, Jack could see smoke starting to fill the room. *They were going to burn the place down, building by building,* thought Jack. He ducked around the corner just as the shotgun barked like a giant rottweiler and bits of plaster flew off the wall where he had stood.

He sprinted to the last of the series of buildings and again slipped behind the northern side to avoid the shooter in the pine trees. Jack peeped around the back edge of the building. He was now sufficiently far to the east to be able to get around the back of the building without the tree shooter seeing him.

Leaning up against the wall was an old Yamaha two-stroke motorcycle, of the off-road kick-start type. It had no lights or indicators and was clearly only used for off-road recreational purposes. In the open field between this building and the distant lake was a long firebreak separating the forest to the south from the one to his north. Someone, probably an employee, had used this firebreak as an off-road track for some stress relieve during lunch breaks or after work.

Jack had considered sprinting into the trees to his north but it meant he would have to cover nearly two hundred meters of open field before reaching the cover of the trees. That presented ample opportunity to the south side shooter to take him out with a shot to his back. He could only see two remaining options now. Either run at an oblique angle to the southern side trees and hope that the shooter would miss a target running across his field of fire, or, he could try this motorcycle and head off down the firebreak to the lake at the bottom of the run. Jack made his split second choice, *try the motorcycle, give the kick-starter at least five attempts then if still not started, run like hell for the south side trees but aim for a spot about one hundred and fifty meters down the firebreak to put some distance between him and the shooter*.

The motor-cycle started on the second kick and made a deafening high-pitched racket, like someone rapidly shaking big ball bearings in a tin can… on steroids. Jack spun the bike around and it took off like a bat out of hell as soon as the engine revs reached its power band. He had owned a four-stroke motorcycle before but nothing close to the power of the monster beneath him. It did not seem to have much control of the power either, with an all or nothing response to the throttle. If he tried to slow down it almost died, when he allowed it to build revs it just took off at full power again.

He had not noticed if anyone was still shooting at him, it took all his attention to keep this mad motorcycle from hurling him into the forest at full speed. He sped up a small incline only to have his stomach turn as the ground dropped away beneath the motorcycle and he and the machine started to descend towards the earth again. Jack braced for the impact but the motorcycles shock absorbers did their job and he felt like he had been dropped onto a big marshmallow. Then he had to suddenly swerve to avoid a big rock dead ahead and another soon after.

Tears streamed down his cheeks as the wind blasted through his face. He could feel adrenalin pumping like never before then just as quickly as it began, it was over. The motorcycle spluttered and died and he free wheeled the last fifty or so meters to the lake edge where he dropped the motorcycle and ran on very shaky legs into the trees on the north side of the firebreak.

Jack paused for breath once he was in the cover of the trees. He was more terrified as a result of that motor-cycle dash down the mountain than he was from being shot at. He could at least control his body and try to avoid being shot but that bloody mad motor-cycle was a trip he would sooner forget than repeat.

I have to get to Sydney! thought Jack, getting frustrated with his situation. He looked around him to try to figure a new plan of action. He could see the lake water through the trees but in all other directions was just more trees.

He decided to make his way around the lake to the dam wall he had caught a brief glimpse of a few moments earlier when he was flying through the air on the motorcycle. There had to be an access road there to somewhere civilized where he could get transport.

Golakov and Todorova drove up to the security guard at Cooper and Sons in Wallerwang. They were intending to kill everyone here and burn the place down. Their ASIO mole was tapped into the security camera feeds at the fireworks factory and had tipped him off that Jack had shown up a few minutes ago. He was too close, way to close and unfortunately it meant that they had to destroy the place.

Golakov got out of his car as the security guard approached and grabbed him by the throat and in one movement, lifted him off the ground, swung his feet into the air and slammed the back of the security guards head into the concrete pavement next to him. It made a satisfying crunching popping sound. Golakov was pleased and made a mental note to record the sound the next time he killed someone that way. It would make a good sound effect for pushing soft-keys on his mobile phone.

Blood began trickling out of the back of the head into the gutter then Golakov noticed a brown stain appearing on the road by the guards buttocks. The body had involuntarily crapped itself upon death. He wondered about that for a few moments. What survival purpose was served by having the body do such a foul act upon death. It did not happen every time but he had killed enough people to know that it happened quite often. He had decided it was a weakness of character. Surely he, Golakov, would never permit himself to do that when he died a hero's death. He sucked in snot from his sinuses and spat on the dead security guard.

There were usually two security guards there, one at the gate and the other paroling the premises. They took turns working the gate and rotated every two hours or so. Todorova took a rifle from behind the seat and began making his way through the trees on the south side of the factory. He was to shoot Jack on sight as his primary target and shoot the other security guard as secondary target. After that it was targets of opportunity, kill anything that moved.

Golakov opened the main gate and drove in to the parking area where Jack had parked but he made sure not to park too close to Jack's new rented car. He open the trunk and took out a home-made flamethrower which he strapped onto his back. Then he took out a shotgun and clipped the flamethrower nozzle to the bottom of the shotgun. This was a good day, thought Golakov. Shooting people with a shotgun and burning them as they lay dying was something he loved. The bodies would sometimes twitch and make funny movements as the flames took hold and if they crapped themselves it was just more fuel to the fire.

He walked up to Jack's car and broke the side window with the shotgun then squeezed the trigger on the flamethrower. A burning sticky fuel mixture squirted into the car and bright yellow flames quickly filled the interior. Next was the admin building. He kicked open the front door and walked through the building looking for people but found none. It was disappointing but he knew they were here somewhere and he would get to them soon. He went back to the furthest room and started throwing flames into each admin room then he exited back out the front door because flames were already licking at the back door area.

Golakov walked around the admin building and turned the corner just in time to see the second security guard walking towards the entrance of the second building. The guard had all his attention on the door he was approaching and was oblivious of Golakov approaching from behind. Just as he began to open the door, Golakov shot him in the back and he fell right in front of the door. Golakov silently cursed himself for not firing a second sooner, before the guard got to the door because now the body was blocking the door. He grabbed the body by the ankle and began dragging it backwards, smiling at how the man's head bobbed up and down as his chin caught and scrapped on the stony surface and then it made an audible clink as a one of his front teeth caught and broke off.

He dropped the man's foot then opened the door fully, just in time to see Jack scurrying around like a cockroach on the other end of the long room. In front of him, a few meters from the door lay the body of one of the managers, shot by Todorova. Golakov shut the door behind him and set fire to it to make sure Jake could not get out that way. He walked up to the body on the floor, stepped over it and set fire to it and took a moment to enjoy the spectacle before turning around and heading for the back where he had seen Jack.

When he got there he found that Jack had escaped through a trap door in the floor so he shot the lock off the back door and kicked it open. He laughed as he saw Jack hiding around the corner of the next building. What a coward. He shot a round in his direction but the little rabbit of a man had run off just in time.

'Come fight me like a man you fucking coward,' yelled Golakov. He turned around and shot another blast of sticky fuel into the building to make sure it burnt well then he went down the stairs and kicked in the door of the next building and set fire to it as well. By the time he was finished with the last building he had lost sight of Jack altogether. He walked over to the fence on the south where he met Todorova who told him he had spotted Jack going down the firebreak on a motorcycle but had not managed to shoot him because he was going too fast and changing speed all the time making it difficult to predict his path and shoot with accuracy.

Golakov was pissed off with Todorova's incompetence so he told him to head down the south side of the firebreak on foot and try to pick up Jack's trail on that side of the lake. Golakov walked back up to the car park and opened a map book of the area. If Jack followed the lake edge on the northern side of the firebreak he would eventually reach the stream that fed the lake and would probably follow it upstream for two kilometers until he got to the road bridge where he would flag down a passing car. Golakov decided to go wait for him at the road bridge but first he made a phone call to his ASIO contact and requested a police sniffer dog be sent to pick up Jack's trail from where he had left the motorcycle.

Golakov parked some distance away from the road bridge and then took his shotgun and his flamethrower into the forest with him. He wiped his prints off the flamethrower and then hid it in a hollow and piled some rocks and leaves on top of it. When he got to the stream he looked around and found a suitable hiding spot which gave him a clear view of the stream for some distance. Then he waited.

After about thirty minutes he heard a helicopter approach and land somewhere to the west of him. Jack would probably be coming up the stream within the next ten to fifteen minutes by his estimate so put his mobile phone onto silent and stayed alert. A few minutes later he received a text message from Todorova saying:

Path blocked by cliff. If he came this way then he must have swum past.

Golakov fumed and typed his reply: *Then start swimming!*

He waited another thirty minutes then realized that Jack had perhaps not come this way or he may have followed the stream for a while then taken another route. Golakov sent a text message to his ASIO contact: *Need an update on the dog team.* Ten minutes later he received his reply: *Sniffer dog still on trail. Lost it briefly at the stream but picked it up again on edge of lake*. Golakov realized that Jack was not coming up the stream as he had expected so he got up and headed back to his car. He wondered how it was that luck seemed to follow this ASIO rabbit named Jack. Todorova had gone south around the lake but Jack had gone north. He had not come up the stream as expected but had continued on around the far side of the lake. It made no sense to Golakov. This Jack character seemed quite logical half the time but he was very unpredictable and lucky the rest of the time.

At the car, he took out his map and checked the far side of the lake. What was Jack's plan, assuming he had one. He was probably just running scared. Golakov followed the lake edge and saw that it had a small dam wall and beyond that was the main road to Lithgow. It was possible that Jack was simply backtracking on the other side of the lake to make everyone think he had gone up the stream when he was actually going downstream to the main road, hoping to hitch a ride back to Lithgow.

Golakov phoned his ASIO contact and said, 'He's heading for the Great Western Highway. You need to set up road blocks in both directions from the dam wall.'

'Sure, but we have limited police presence in the area. It's a bloody small town you know. We had to fly the dog in from Katoomba on a private helicopter.'

'Well get that helicopter back in the air with a policeman in it and start looking,' said Golakov.

'I already dispatched two military helicopters with two more dogs from our military base at Holsworthy. ETA twenty minutes.'

'Tell them shoot to kill. We can't fuck around with this Jack ass any longer,' said Golakov.

'How did he get past you two geniuses?'

'Don't get smart with me you prick. Just do your fucking job,' said Golakov then ended the call, suppressing an urge to smash it to pieces on the ground.

He looked back at the map and worked out the shortest road route to the dam wall.

It had taken Jack about an hour and a half to negotiate his way around the lake edge to the dam wall. He had crossed the stream which fed the lake but had not bothered to follow it upstream. It was too obvious a choice and he would be an easy target for someone lying in ambush further up the stream.

At the dam wall he could see a dirt road leading from there to a tarred road in the distance. Jack started heading for the tar road but then something caught his eye, flashing lights... red and blue flashing lights.

He strained his eyes and could just make out what appeared to be a police road-block about eight hundred meters along the road towards Lithgow. The guy with the shotgun must have recognized him as himself, Jack, without the wig, and must have tipped off police that a wanted fugitive bomb maker had just set fire to a firework factory. His enemies were making it really difficult for him to get to Sydney and tip-off someone about the radioactive fireworks.

Jack had already considered what he would say to police when he got there. *Could he even trust them?* His enemies seemed to have influence within police and ASIO and they would probably have him killed soon after he was captured. *Shot while fleeing police custody* was how he imagined the newspaper headline would read.

He decided against it. He could not take his news to the police and expect them to stop the new years fireworks display. It was up to him to get there and do what ever he had to, to prevent those fireworks from going off.

On the other side of the tar road was more pine forest. If he could make it in there then he might be able to work his way around the road block and rejoin the tar road some distance beyond the road block where he could hitch a ride with a passing motorist. There was one possible problem though. He had attended a police road block before as an ASIO agent when they where doing a man hunt for another fugitive. He had seen police search the vehicles but more importantly, they had shown pictures of the wanted man to the motorists specifically to prevent the fugitive from becoming a hitch-hiker. He did not know if it had been a one time thing or if it was standard police practice to show photos of the wanted person. He decided it was better to assume the worst and avoid trying to hitch a ride.

High tension power lines ran past the lake about one hundred and fifty meters from him in the direction of the road block. The power lines then crossed the tar road and cut through the pine forest in the direction of Lithgow. Jack knew that all power lines would have a dirt road underneath them to allow workers to gain access to the line for repairs and maintenance. It was like a dirt highway with no police road blocks and hidden from the busy tar road. He knew he could run the ten kilometers to

Lithgow in about sixty minutes. It was not optimum but for now he did not have a better idea.

A distant sound of a helicopter brought Jack back to reality. He looked back over the lake in the direction of the sound and could just make out some activity on the far lake shore where the mad motor-cycle was lying in the grass. It was too far to see clearly but it looked as if the police had brought a dog to sniff his trail through the forest.

It would not take them long to figure out which way he was going and then send another dog to try to pick up his scent here at the dam wall. He figured he had about fifteen to twenty minutes before a dog team showed up here. *Oh crap!*, thought Jack. He had to act fast. No matter what he did now, he could not head straight to an obvious destination. The police would use the dogs to figure out his general direction and then make an educated guess about his intended destination. They would then send an ahead team to ambush him if he showed up there. It was a well-tested tactic which had captured many fugitives in the past.

Golakov drove along the winding road through the pine forest until it joined the Great Western Highway, then he turned south and headed towards Lithgow. As he neared the lake he turned off onto a dirt track and then parked his vehicle out of sight from anyone near the dam wall. He made his way through the trees until he saw a familiar figure crouching behind a log among the trees near the dam wall. He approached as quietly as possibly but as he drew near, Todorova spoke up and said, 'I hear your elephant steps from a long way off Golakov.'

'I wasn't trying to sneak up on you,' said Golakov gruffly. 'Have you seen that prick yet?'

'I saw some movement in the trees on the other side of the dam wall. I also heard a dog barking from further up. I figure they will flush him out of the trees and then I will shoot him,' said Todorova. Golakov knew that if Todorova shot Jack within sight of the police dog unit then they would have to kill the policemen as well. No loose ends.

They waited and watched and after a while saw two policemen emerge from the trees with a sniffer dog. All three of them looked tired and flustered. Tracking through a forest full of boulders and fallen trees was no simple task and it had taken its toll. Golakov watched as they followed the dog to the water's edge then the policemen split up, one looking for visible signs of an exit point in one direction while the other used the dog to try to pick up the trail in the other direction.

Golakov began to realize that Jack must have heard the dog or assumed that they would put a dog on his trail and had taken appropriate measures. He had gone into the lake and depending on how far he could swim, he could emerge anywhere on the vast circumference of the lake shore. Even with two extra sniffer dogs on the way it was going to be a very difficult and time-consuming task to pick up Jack's trail again.

Todorova gave Golakov a questioning look as they began to hear the sound of heavy helicopter blades approaching.

'Our friend send two more dogs and some military troops,' said Golakov. 'We should leave now.'

They both crept away quietly and went back to where Golakov had parked his vehicle.

Jack realized that he had to cover his tracks to try to confuse the sniffer dogs. He turned and headed for the lake, walking right into the water then stopped. His plan was that once the dogs had picked up his trail they would follow it to the water's edge where it would look like his plan was to swim some distance and emerge somewhere else on the shore.

It was a good plan but the dogs would be made to search the lake shore in both directions until they re-acquired his scent at the point where he emerged and then they would be back on his trail. The other problem was that a man swimming in a lake would be highly visible from the shore and from a helicopter. He was actually surprised that a police helicopter had not shown up yet. They would probably send one from Sydney soon enough.

Jack turned, exited the lake and followed his own trail back to the forest he had emerged from. He kept his eye on the trees above him and soon found what he was looking for. A low branch.

He jumped with all his strength and caught hold of it then swung his legs up and onto the branch then pulled himself up to a sitting position. He then moved along the branch to the tree trunk, climbed around it to another branch going in the opposite direction then moved out along that branch until it thinned enough to dip down, threatening to break. Jack dropped to the ground and moved off in a direction perpendicular to his original trail.

The plan now was that the dogs would waste time looking for a trail along the lake shore. If they gave up and followed the trail he had walked it would seem to be intact all the way from the motorcycle to the dam wall. His escape into the tree was therefore invisible to the sniffer dogs because the trail on the ground would be unbroken. The only possible way to find his new trail was to search at a distance along both sides of his original trail, a mammoth task which would buy him all the time he needed.

###

Golakov drove off onto the Great Western Highway just as two large military helicopters landed in the cleared space near the dam wall. He knew they would eventually find Jack's trail and with sixteen armed soldiers to help, they would have a good chance of catching him. He also knew that Jack had a good head start and it was just possible that he had managed to slip past the road block and was heading to Sydney. They figured that Jack now knew about the plan they had made with mixing the radioactive dust into the fireworks. Jack would try to get to Sydney and warn the authorities, so they had to find him and kill him as soon as possible.

He dropped Todorova off near the entrance to Lithgow and told him to find a spot where he could cover both the train line and the road. Golakov drove on towards the station and found a parking spot which gave him a good view of the station entrance and the platform. If Jack had managed to get a lift to Lithgow he would probably catch a train to Sydney to try to avoid any further road blocks on the road. Golakov was ready for him.

Jack was now headed in the general direction of the roadblock he had seen earlier but he was moving parallel with the tar road and about one hundred meters away from it, surrounded by pine trees. He did not have a specific plan other than putting some distance between himself and the dogs. He just hoped that as he progressed, another opportunity would present itself.

The slope of the land began to rise and Jack noticed that the road to his right was curving away from him. By now he had moved past the police road block so he started moving to his right as well to keep track with the road. Suddenly he heard the loud rumble of a train up ahead. The sound had started abruptly and had not built up as the train approached. He figured it had to be a train tunnel.

He ran towards the sound and after about twenty seconds he almost fell on top of a long coal train exiting a tunnel directly beneath him. He had to think fast. He had no idea how long the train was. It could end abruptly and then he would miss his chance. Jack readied himself and felt his body resist his will as he forced it to enter a dangerous situation. He jumped just as the start of a coal car exited the mouth of the tunnel and by the time he landed, he was just past the middle of the carriage and sliding rapidly to the rear.

The coal consisted of golf ball sized chunks which did not give a great deal of friction and resisted Jack efforts to stop his slide. He went off the back edge and at the last instant he managed to grab hold of the metal rim at the rear of the carriage. To his left were several metal brackets protruding from the carriage which served as a crude ladder.

Jack, hanging from the back of the carriage, moved hand of hand until he could reach the top rung of the carriage ladder where he managed to gain some security. He climbed down to the lowest rung and then hung on. The train line ran parallel with the road for a while leaving Jack feeling quite exposed but fortunately he was on the far side of the carriage and would be rather difficult to spot.

Day suddenly turned to night as the train entered another tunnel. The reflected noise off the tunnel walls was deafening. Eventually the sky came back as the train exited the tunnel and Jack felt the sun burn against his neck. The train seemed to be hugging a mountain on his left but on the other side of the carriage Jack could see farmland and beyond that was a tarred road, probably the Great Western Highway.

After a while the housing density increased and as he looked past the edge of the carriage, he saw they were approaching Lithgow where he assumed the train would stop.

He was mistaken however, the train only slowed slightly and Lithgow was there and gone in a matter of seconds. He had wanted to get off and use road transport which would have been quicker than a comparatively slow coal train, but now he was stuck on the train.

Jack assumed that this train was headed to the industrial harbor at Newcastle but at the speed it was going it would take four or five hours to get there. *Not good enough*, thought Jack. Another problem was that the train was probably not going to stop at any stations along the way because it was not a regular goods train.

Chapter 12

Randy was unhappy about being at work on 31 December. The rest of Sydney was in a festive holiday mood but he and the other ASIO staff assigned to the train crash case had to go to work. Crime did not take holidays.

Right now he was sitting on a toilet seat with his pants down. He had used his personal mobile phone to check and update the secure server which Jack had set up and this was the safest place he could find in a pinch.

It was 2:00 PM and still no news from Jack. This morning he had sent him a list of companies which used the chemicals he had found and he assumed Jack was still in Lithgow going around to all the companies on the list to try to get a lead. It was probably a lot more interesting than the work he was doing in the office.

An alert message suddenly flashed on Randy's phone. He opened it and started reading then felt himself go cold as a fear grabbed a hold. The message informed him that someone from the ASIO office had accessed the log file on the secure server. The actual secure messages were not at risk because they were encrypted but the log file showed the I.P addresses of people who used the server.

What scared Randy was that it was someone from *this* ASIO office. It could not be coincidence that they had chosen that particular server to check out of all the millions of others on the internet. It could also not be coincidence that they had checked now, while he was away from his desk in the toilet. Everyone in the office was busy checking up on the train crash case which meant that the only way someone could have arrived at his secure server was if they were looking for it specifically.

The only electronic trail which led to the secure server came from his personal phone and the two mobiles operating under the name of Renae's uncle. Someone had violated his privacy and illegally accessed or obtained his phone records. Whoever it was, was on to him and he needed to get out of there.

Randy exited the toilet cubicle just as Crowley walked in to the toilet area.

'Oh there you are,' said Crowley. 'I was looking for you.' He glared at Randy as if he was an unwanted cockroach in a cupboard.

'Sorry, I ate something that did not agree and it has been rough.' Crowley was blocking the door with his big body so Randy went to the hand basin and began washing his hands.

'It's been happening a lot this week,' said Crowley with a hint of sarcasm and a bit too much confidence. Randy ignored the comment and finished washing his hands. Crowley approached the basins at a slow pace and said,

'You not gonna answer me? I know what you really been doing you shit head.' His tone was low and menacing and Randy knew the game was up. Crowley was probably the one who obtained his phone records. He certainly had the security clearance to do something like that. It was also probably Crowley who had deleted the report about the Aboriginal in Adelaide. Randy realized that Crowley was probably going to trace the other two I.P address and eventually discover that Renae also knew what was going on. He had to get out of there and warn her and Jack.

He decided to try one last bluff. He only knew one Karate move and he had to take a chance and try or he was probably going to be taking a one way ride in the trunk of Crowley's car.

'Sorry boss, I was just wondering why someone would throw a perfectly good mobile phone into the bin,' said Randy while pointing at the rubbish bin next to the basin. It worked, Crowley's attention was momentarily misdirected and Randy chose that moment to shoot his knee up to waist height while simultaneously kicking his lower leg outwards.

He had no idea what the move was called but he had practiced it once or twice and knew it delivered a blazingly fast and powerful kick without having to learn weird spin kicks or round-house whatevers.

His foot flew into Crowley's groin, delivering a blow that instantly turned Crowley's face a deathly shade of grey as his knees started to collapse and he sank to the ground. Randy figured he had better do a proper job so he did his kick maneuver again. Crowley was already on his knees so the blow caught him under the chin and snapped his head back, then Crowley fell over to the ground on his side, his heading landing in the trough of the wall urinal.

Randy quickly stepped over him and went out the door, heading straight for the exit. He was shaking from the effects of the adrenaline rush mixed with the fear of the unknown. He could almost not believe it had worked. He also had no idea how long Crowley would be down for, probably not long at all, and when he got up he would be *really* pissed at Randy.

The security guard at the exit eyed Randy curiously and said, 'Everything okay mate? You look a bit pale.'

'Uhm… yeah, I just been looking at too many pictures of dead bodies from that train crash. I need to get some fresh air.'

'Yeah, that can wear you down…' said the guard, trying to sound like he was a war veteran.

Randy did not bother going for his car in the parking garage. He figured they knew what it looked like and would be looking for it on the streets. He doubted he would even make it out of the parking garage. If Crowley sounded the alarm then all exits including the parking garage would be instantly locked. His quickest route outside was via the connecting passage into the underground train station next to the Town Hall. As soon as he turned the corner and was out of site of the security guard, he sprinted for the door then used his security ID to open it and walk out through what appeared to be a maintenance door into the masses of people in the public areas of the station.

Thirty kilometers south-east of Lithgow, Jack was still clinging onto the metal ladder at the end of the coal carriage. The train had wound its way around more hills and through more tunnels and it would have been a much more pleasant experience were it not for the fact that Jack was desperate to get off and find a quicker form of transport.

The train was slowing down again which meant it was going to be passing through another small town station. Just then, a movement in the sky caught his attention and he looked up to see a purple bi-plane flying low and it appeared to be descending as if on a landing approach. It flew directly over the train and then he lost sight of it just as the train entered the small town of Medlow. Jack recalled having seen the Medlow road sign just five kilometers beyond Katoomba... and ... he recalled the advert on the wall at the Scenic Railway. Katoomba had an airfield.

Jack decided to take his chances and try to get to the airfield. The ground next to the train track was flat and covered in grass and the train was going as slow as it was ever going to, so he had maybe a minute or two before it began picking up speed again. He poked his head around the carriage and looked forward. The flat grassy area was coming to an end and would be replaced by trees and bushes. If he jumped off and hit a tree he would probably break an arm or a leg. He had to go now.

The landing in the grass was harder than he was expecting and too fast to stay on his feet. He fell over and slid several meters before coming to rest an arm's length away from the first of the trees. Fortunately there had been no glass or other sharp objects in the grass or he may have been badly injured or cut. He lay there for a second or two, looking around to see if anyone had seen his jump. The coast appeared to be clear so he stood up and walked around the back of the tree and leaned up against it, pretending to be a casual train enthusiast watching the train go by.

He waited for the last few carriages to go by then tried to get his bearings. The tree he was leaning against was a pine tree, one of several which formed a tree-lined avenue in a part of Medlow which bordered the train line. Four hundred meters back along the train track was Medlow train station. On the other side of the train line was a much busier tar road, the Great Western Highway and two hundred meters back along that road was a building with a sign outside saying Hydro Majestic Hotel.

It was a very unusual looking building with one part having a square domed roof and the section next to it having a crenelated parapet on top, giving the structure a middle eastern appearance. It looked posh enough to make Jack suspect that some of its guests might be arriving by private airplane.

He decided to go over to the hotel and ask about the airfield.

###

After waiting at the station for an hour Golakov began to get annoyed. He called their ASIO mole and asked, 'Any news on your fucking rogue agent?'

'Nothing yet. The fresh dogs circled the lake but found no exit point. The helicopters and the troops have searched the area but got nothing so far. I told you I'd call when we knew something.'

'I'm coming to Sydney,' said Golakov. 'He's going to try to sabotage our efforts and we need to stop him.'

'I've assigned all the police in Sydney to patrol the area and keep an eye on the fireworks. If he shows up they have orders to shoot to kill'

'I'm coming anyway,' said Golakov.

'Then stay the fuck out of my way,' said their contact. 'If you get caught I can't help you.'

Golakov started the engine and went off to pick up Todorova.

'Good Afternoon Sir. How can we help you today?' asked the friendly desk clerk. Her name tag read Miranda.

'Hello Miranda,' said Jack. He was aware that she had noticed his somewhat soiled jeans and T-shirt. She was unlikely to consider him a potential guest. Then again, this was Australian mountain country. He could easily be a bush walker back from a morning hike through the valley behind the hotel. He decided to go with the last option.

'I'm supposed to meet up with my mates for a scenic flight along the ridge line but I got delayed in the valley.' Then pointing at the dirt marks on his clothes he added, 'My fault really, I got sidetracked off the path and ended up having to fight my way through thick bush before I reconnected with the path again.'

She seemed impressed and said, 'Wow, you certainly are brave. I would not want to try something like that.'

'Oh it wasn't too bad,' said Jack modestly. 'I was following the stream and knew the walking path would be on my right below the ridge, so when I was done I just headed for the ridge. Simple enough but not as clean as the walking path.'

'Oh I see. So what brings you to the hotel?'

'Well, I was supposed to met my mates in front of the hotel. I see that they have already left so I need a ride out to the airfield rather urgently.' Jack took a fifty dollar note out of his pocket. He knew that the airfield could not be more than five or ten minutes drive away. Fifty dollars would be five times the going rate. He waved the fifty in front of her and said 'I'll give this fifty to whoever can get me to the airfield in the next ten minutes.'

She winked at Jack and took the fifty, saying, 'I'll see what I can do for you.' She disappeared through a door behind the reception area and a few moments later she reappeared saying, 'Benny will be with you shortly.'

'Thank you,' said Jack then looking around at the beautiful foyer area he added. 'This hotel sure is beautiful. It must have an interesting history.'

Miranda followed his gaze and said, 'Yes, it's nice. It opened in 1904. Did you know that Sir Arthur Conan Doyle, creator of Sherlock Holmes stayed here once?'

'Really? I had no idea. That's amazing.' He admired the beautiful decorations and found himself thinking of Renae. She would love it here. He would love being here with her.

A young fellow, probably nineteen years old came to him looking flustered and asked, 'You the guy going to the airfield?'

'Yes...'

'Okay, this way please.' Jack followed him outside to the end of the parking area and was shown to an old yellow Volkswagen Beetle, obviously Benny's personal car. Jack strongly suspected that Miranda had offered him only ten dollars and kept the fifty for herself.

The old Beetle bounced along the dirt road to the airfield as it wound through the lush green forest, slowly making its way up the hill to the plateau on top where the airfield lay. The surrounding trees ensured that the airfield remained hidden until they drove onto the edge of it and stopped. Jack saw two white Cessna's and the purple biplane parked not too far away on the side of the grass strip. The landing strip itself seemed like an amateur production compared to the airfields he had seen at Oak Fields and Maralinga. The runway here was actually somewhat concave as it followed the curve of the plateau and it appeared to have not been surface compressed or hardened in any way.

Jack's keen eye was attracted to the purple biplane. He recognized it as a Pitts Special used for performing aerial stunts at air shows. A man was busy with it and appeared to be preparing it for flight. Another group of about five people were standing around one of the two Cessna aeroplanes. Jack thanked Benny then headed for the group of aeroplanes. As he approached the group of people he realized that they were tourists about to embark on a scenic flight. The pilot was giving his pre-flight talk, explaining some safety details. Jack greeted them and continued walking to the biplane. He had doubts about his ability to convince a bunch of tourists to abandon their scenic flight so that he could go to Sydney.

'Nice plane,' said Jack.

The man turned to see who was speaking then said, 'Afternoon mate.' He stuck out his hand and said, 'Phil's the name.' There was something open and honest about this man that Jack liked.

'Jack,' said Jack then realized he had just told the man his real name.

'So you like it then?' said Phil gesturing proudly at his biplane.

'It's a beauty,' said Jack with genuine admiration. The name of the plane, *Royal Passion*, was written in white over the engine cowling.

'I brought it all the way from Perth just for the show this afternoon. They specifically wanted a purple stunt plane because of the Royal visit. You prolly heard about William and Kate being in Sydney, right? Damn east coast guys get all the big knobs. Nobody important bothers going to Perth.'

'That's not totally true,' said Jack warmly. 'You Perth guys have the Red Bull air race event every year.'

'Oh yeah...' laughed Phil. 'We beat you on that one. Sydney's got too much valuable real-estate along the harbor area. Nobody wanted to risk a stunt plane crashing into the Opera House or the Harbor Bridge.'

'So are you putting on a show this afternoon?' asked Jack.

'Yes sir!' said Phil proudly. 'I'm going to wow the afternoon crowd who've been gathering for the fireworks. Just heading that way now then coming back here to spend the night at the Hydra.'

Jack decided to get a bit more serious and said, 'Phil, I'll pay you handsomely for a lift into Sydney. I need to get there urgently and can't afford to wait the two or three hours that it's going to take by car.'

Phil looked at Jack then realized he was not joking. He seemed to ponder the situation for a few moments then said, 'Well I can drop you at Bankstown airport, but that will have to be after I do my show cause if I leave now I'll get there on schedule but I can't be late. Sydney Major won't be impressed if I keep William and Kate waiting.'

'Thank you,' said Jack, then asked. 'Can I borrow your mobile phone?'

Randy was walking through the busy underground shopping area which ran all the way from Town Hall to Martin Place. He was desperately trying to formulate a plan of action. He now effectively had no car and no home to go to. Crowley would surely accuse him of working with a known fugitive which meant that he had also just become a wanted man. Trying to reach his home or car would be a sure way to get caught. He decided to update the secure server one last time then toss his phone, or maybe just toss the sym-card.

He was not keen to toss his phone because of all the software tools he had installed on it. If he just replaced the sym-card, effectively giving himself a new phone number, it was still possible to trace his phone. Sure it would be more difficult but it was possible. All mobile phones had their own digital fingerprint regardless of the phone number provided by the sym-card. It would still be possible to run a trace looking for his phone's digital fingerprint. He knew that the best thing to do was to get a complete new phone... but, for now he decided the best way to be untraceable and still keep his phone for later would be to remove the battery.

Randy's phone started ringing. He had been so deep in thought that it did not immediately register with him that it required some action on his part. He had stopped and stared at it stupidly for a second or two before coming out of his hypnotic state and consciously looked at the phone. It was not a number he was familiar with but he answered it anyway. Fortunately it was Jack.

'Jack, buddy... I'm in shit street here,' said Randy somewhat frantically. 'Crowley is the ASIO mole. I just kicked him and his head landed in the pisser... then I... then I got the fuck outa there. I'm gonna have to dump my phone man... where the fuck are you man?'

'Relax a bit Randy,' said Jack calmly. 'I also got big news. I'm on my way to Sydney, reckon I'll be there in thirty minutes. We need to meet up somewhere...'

'Stop!' yelled Randy. 'Don't mention locations. Crowley managed to get the phone records for this phone and he knows which I.P addresses have looked at the secure server. I'll bet the prick is listening to us right now.'

'Okay, got it, but you need to understand that we are out of time. The problem we were looking into goes down tonight at 8pm... it's in the fireworks...'

'You... you mean...', stammered Randy as he realized what Jack was saying.

'Correct,' said Jack.

'Oh shit Jack, what we gonna do?'

'You know that place we watched those yoga girls working out that time?'

'Yeah... when?'

'Let's make it forty-five minutes to one hour from now. You need to be a bit flexible on that. And another thing...'

'Yeah, what?' asked Randy.

'Find our other friend and bring them along. We gonna need as much help as possible to pull this off,' said Jack to let Randy know to bring Renae to the meeting spot. He also wanted her away from her apartment in case Crowley figured out who the third person was and where they lived.

###

Jack was seated in the front cockpit of the Pitts Special, directly over the wing which unfortunately limited his view of the ground directly below him. They had just arrived over Sydney, having taken a mere thirty minutes to fly from Katoomba at an air speed of nearly three hundred kilometers per hour. Phil circled low over the harbor area to get his bearings and to get the crowd's attention.

Jack used this opportunity to observe the layout and try to formulate a plan of action. He noticed that pyrotechnic mortars had been placed on both arches of the harbor bridge. He also noticed similar mortars along the spines of the two bigger Opera House buildings. A similar array of fireworks were visible on a floating barge in the bay to the east of the Opera House. Fort Denison out in the main harbor channel also appeared to be rigged with fireworks. To the west of the bridge was another small island called Port Jackson. It was probably also rigged with fireworks.

It was going to be a mission to try to get to all those locations and sabotage the fireworks before 8:00PM.

'Here we go,' said Phil as he broke out of his circular flight path and dove for the water. Jack watched as the water rushed towards him, feeling very uncomfortable from having his internal organs and stomach contents suddenly become weightless. Just when he could not take any more, Phil pulled back and brought the plane out of its dive, the intense G-forces pinning Jack in his seat and pulling his face tissue towards the back of his head, exposing his teeth in a stupid grin.

The G-forces eased off as the plane leveled out and the little Pitts Special now hurtled towards the harbor bridge at a speed somewhere between three fifty and four hundred kilometers per hour. Jack saw the Opera House whizz by on his left and then they went under the harbor bridge before Phil brought the plane straight up, going vertical.

Jack had wanted to look out the cockpit but he was unable to move his head, the crushing G-forces had pressed his head solidly into the head rest. Phil eased off on the throttle and the G-forces diminished until Phil turned the rudder and brought the plane around to face the water again. Jack now had that uncomfortable weightless sensation again as the plane started diving back down towards the water on the other side of the bridge. Jack realized that they had effectively looped high over the top of the bridge and were about to swoop down the other side and whizz by the Opera House again. He readied himself but much to his horror, Phil had other plans.

He leveled out in the opposite direction, flying back under the bridge upside down. Jack felt his body weight straining at the harness which held him firmly in his seat. If they snapped he would be launched straight through the canopy of the plane into the harbor water which would probably break his neck on impact.

Phil then did a half roll to bring the plane right side up before doing a tight circle over Berry's Point to wow the crowds who had gathered at Balls Head reserve. He flew back under the north side of the bridge then turned south, heading straight for the gap between the two main structures of the Opera House.

Jack, looking forward, could see a small group of well dressed people gathered outside the top floor harbor side entrance of the Opera House. As they neared he recognized William and Kate and then Phil turned the plane on its side and shot through the gap before making a tight turn all the way around the bay over the Royal Botanical Gardens. Jack, glancing out over his left shoulder as the plane banked, saw a huge crowd in the gardens, waving and cheering as the plane swept past overhead.

For the final part of the routine, Phil took the plane to a higher altitude and did some more barrel rolls, wing overs and loops before, much to Jack's relief, announcing that they were done.

The Pitts Special engine now started to splutter and Phil guided the aircraft towards Centennial Park where he landed in an empty stretch of field to the east of the Eastside Horse Riding Academy. The great thing about the biplane was that the double wings gave it a great deal of lift which translated into it needing only a very short runway for take off and landing. Phil expertly brought the plane to a safe landing in the east end of the field and then Jack got out and opened the engine cover and after a few seconds he closed it again. Phil turned the plane around, opened the throttle and took off heading west over the Centennial Park Restaurant while Jack remained hidden in the trees bordering the park.

Jack had previously arranged this little charade with Phil before leaving Katoomba. He had shown Phil his ASIO ID and told him that the reason for his haste to get to Sydney was because of a very real threat of a terrorist attack on the Royal couple. Bankstown airport was too far from Sydney CBD to suit Jack's time requirements so he had asked Phil to fake an engine problem necessitating an emergency landing. Phil would have to take off again quickly before a crowd of on lookers began to form which might make take-off impossible and draw too much unwanted attention. Jack was now about one and half kilometers from his meeting place with Randy at the Sunken Gardens. A comfortable jog would get him there in ten minutes,

Chapter 13

Jack walked down the long staircase which descended from street level down to the gardens below. The site was well over a hundred years old and had formerly been known as the Paddington Reservoir. Back in the day it had held water for the many new settlers but had eventually been abandoned as a reservoir as the city grew. Eventually part of the roof had collapsed and city engineers had redeveloped it as a beautiful garden area with the remaining brick arches and wooden pillars giving it an odd but pleasant Roman feel. It was also nicely secluded from the busy street above.

There were a few people wandering around, mostly tourists from China but there was no sign of Randy or Renae. Jack knew they would not be standing out in the open so he started walking along the outer perimeter along a corridor of brick arches. As he approached a stairwell in the far corner, a blond women ran out and threw her arms around his neck.

'Jack, I'm so glad you are safe,' said Renae as she squeezed him tight.

'I missed you too,' said Jack.

'Oh get a room you two,' said Randy as he rounded the corner.

'You also want a hug?' asked Jack jokingly.

'I don't swing that way bro,' said Randy pretending to be aloof but he was clearly pleased to see Jack.

Jack looked around to make sure no one was within hearing distance then said, 'Okay, back to business. I caught a ride in from Katoomba in an airplane and the pilot was kind enough to give me a real close view of the harbor area. There are fireworks on the bridge, the Opera House, two islands and a barge. There might be other locations as well but I think those are the main ones. The fireworks guy in Wallerwang said they were triggered from a computer system and digital radio linked to the various locations.' Jack looked directly at Randy and asked, 'Any ideas on how to kill that system… safely?'

Randy thought for a moment then said, 'The way I understand it then is that the timing or sequence of what goes bang when, would all be programmed into a portable computer. They would probably have more than one such controlling computer for when Murphy's Law rears its ugly head. They would want some redundancy ye know.'

'So if we can get to those computers we can stop the event,' said Renae.

'Well yes, but they could be anywhere. If they got radio links then they could be in any one of thousands of locations or hotel rooms overlooking the harbor area,' said Randy.

'Even if we knew where they where, I doubt we would get near those computers anyway,' said Jack. 'Crowley would have gotten the police to guard it to the extreme.'

'Can't we jam the signal somehow?' asked Renae.

Randy shook his head and said, 'No, we would need to know the frequency they were using and then we would need a powerful transmitter… which we don't have.'

'Is it safe for them to use radio links to the fireworks, I mean, won't mobile phones or lightning strikes and so on cause an accidental triggering of the event?' asked Jack.

Randy shook his head again, 'They would have thought of that. My guess is that whatever gets transmitted would be digitally signed and encrypted and each receiver would only respond to something that matches the digital signature it's programmed for. It would be impossible to falsely trigger such a system.'

'Can't we trip the power-grid somehow, that would stop the equipment from working surely?' asked Renae.

'It might but my educated guess is that they would be using battery backup,' said Randy. 'If I had an annual million dollar fireworks contract I sure would not risk it falling flat in the event of a power failure.'

'It would also take too long to set up. We would need explosives to blow up several substations around the CBD plus those on the north shore as well,' said Jack, then shrugging he added, 'and I don't even know where the substations are.'

'Well we do know where the receivers would be,' said Randy with a big grin.

'What do you mean?' asked Jack.

'You mentioned all the places where you saw fireworks… well, the receivers would be there too, close by… somewhere,' said Randy looking a bit guilty.

Renae was quick to pick up on Randy's reason for holding back. She looked at Jack and said, 'He's telling us we got to climb the bloody bridge and the Opera House!'

'Shit,' said Jack. 'I was hoping for a better way. This means we gonna have to split up. You guys up for it?'

'I don't do well with heights,' said Randy.

'That's okay,' said Jack. 'I was thinking that Crowley has probably given descriptions of you and I to the cops which means we won't get anywhere near the Opera House without a good disguise, which I don't have.' He looked at Renae and said, 'I'll take the bridge, you do the Opera House.' He looked at Randy and said, 'That leaves the two harbor islands and the barge for you. You will need to, uhm, borrow a boat somehow.'

'I'll figure it out,' said Randy. 'Some advice, you guys will need to find the battery packs then rip or cut the wires which lead from there to the receivers. There might also be more than one receiver at each site.'

Renae noticed that Jack had not moved despite having reached an apparent solution, so she asked, 'What's the problem Jack?'

Jack looked at her for a moment then looked back at the ground in front of him. After a lengthy pause he said, 'I just can't see us pulling this off without hurting some innocent people before getting killed ourselves. The bridge access points will be guarded and locked. I would have to somehow knock out the police guarding the place. Once I do that I'm stuck with the problem of trying to hide one or two unconscious policemen. Even if I manage to get past the locked gates onto the top of the bridge arch without alerting anyone, I'm going to be highly visible up there.' He looked at Renae and continued, 'Same with you trying to get onto the Opera House roof. It's impossible to do without at least some climbing equipment... ropes... you won't get near there without drawing attention. If you do by some miracle manage to get onto the roof, you will also be very noticeable up there. Police sharp-shooters will fire if they think someone is a genuine security threat. By now they will assume we are somehow linked to that train explosion and Crowley would probably have issued shoot to kill orders based on the train bombing scam. We need a better plan.'

'I know it sounds extreme but what if we force the Mayor to cancel the fireworks, threaten her if she won't listen to reason,' said Randy.

'That could work,' said Jack, 'Nobody will be guarding her… unless she's hanging out with the royal couple, which may well be the case. Give me a few secs to think on it.' After a moment or two he said, 'We need intel, communication, Internet access and so on. We are working blind right now. We need to at least find out where the Mayor is before we can decide whether that plan is feasible.'

'I have contacts in the media who would know how to contact the Mayor,' said Renae.

Jack said nothing, he was staring at the ground in front of him again.

'You thought of another problem, haven't you?' said Renae.

'Yes… ' said Jack. 'I suspect that the people Crowley is working with would not leave something like this to chance. They have planned this for months and probably have their own computer to trigger the firework event. If we do manage to get someone to call off the event it would only serve to alert them that their scheme has been uncovered.'

'They would probably then trigger the fireworks prematurely to prevent anyone from fiddling with the receivers or fireworks?' asked Renae.

'That's what I think,' said Jack. 'Whatever method we come up with it's going to have to be extremely stealthy. If Crowley even catches sight of one of us near the fireworks he might go ahead and trigger the event prematurely.'

Jack stared at the ground for another few moments then turned to Randy and asked, 'Can we track Crowley's phone somehow, find out where he is?'

'You think he has one of those portable computers?' asked Renae.

'Well yeah, if not, he would surely know something about it or where it is. I'm quite happy to take a baseball bat and beat the crap out of him till he talks. We would be saving thousands of lives. Once we know that they can't trigger the event then it would be safe to get the Mayor to pull the plug on the event from her end.'

'You're assuming that Cooper and Sons aren't involved in some way and they would listen to the Mayor,' said Randy.

'Yes,' said Jack. 'From what I saw in Wallerwang, Cooper and Sons had no clue that the purple mixture was radioactive. I'm convinced that they would shut down the event from their side if the order came from the Mayor or the police chief.'

Jack and Renae were now both looking at Randy expectantly. 'Uhm… well, I could try hacking into his phone and reading his GPS without his knowledge, but it would mean I'd have to switch my iPad back on and they would zero in on our location quite rapidly,' said Randy.

'Can't you switch off the GPS on your iPad, I'm sure I saw something for that in the setting's menu?' asked Renae.

'Yeah, but government agencies like ASIO have back-door access to bypass whatever menu setting you have,' said Randy.

'So much for privacy…' said Renae with disgust.

'Yeah, they justify it with National Security excuses. If you got nothing to hide you got nothing to worry about, and so on,' said Randy.

'We can take my car and drive around the back streets while Randy hacks into Crowley's phone,' said Renae.

'Afraid not,' said Jack. 'You car is too visible and they could still close in on us and block us off with a few police cars. Five, maybe ten minutes tops and they would have us.'

'I have another idea,' said Randy. 'My Toshiba notebook has all the hacking tools I need. The only other thing I would need is Internet access and I could hack in via his data connection. I was going to use my iPad as a WIFI hub for the notebook but if I can find another open WIFI hotspot then I could safely do the hack. Well... fairly safely anyway. Crowley is quite computer savvy. He probably has intrusion detection on his phone.'

'You mean he could trace the intrusion back to the location of the WIFI hotspot?' asked Renae.

'Yes,' said Randy grimly.

'I think I know how to solve that,' said Jack, then pointing at a grounds keeper working on one of the water features he said, 'That bloke is going to have to help us out a bit.' Then he walked off in the direction of the person he had indicated.

Renae looked perplexed at Randy and said, 'I suppose we had better follow him then.'

The grounds keeper led them through a metal gate to a solid metal door which he unlocked. Once inside he switched on a light and Jack saw that they were inside a small tunnel, about two meters high by two meters wide. It was currently being used to store gardening tools and various bits of maintenance equipment, including several flashlights. The tunnel seemed to be leading off in a north-westerly direction but it had another metal gate blocking access to the rest of the tunnel beyond the storage area.

'Thanks mate,' said Jack. 'If you can leave the keys with me I'll lock up and get the keys back to you later.'

'Alright,' said the grounds keeper and then he left them.

Jack turned to Randy and Renae and said, 'Okay, here's the plan. This tunnel used to take the water from this reservoir to the early settler houses at the harbor. When the reservoir shut down they used part of the tunnel as a storm water drain. It runs all the way into the CBD and joins up with various other old storm water tunnels. One of them, the Benelong Drain, runs right under the Opera House into the harbor. Above us, along the way, will be many shops, cafe's and so on. I'll bet that somewhere along this tunnel we can find an open WIFI hotspot. If Crowley traces our hack, his goons can waste their time searching all the building around the hot spot and they won't find us.'

'That's brilliant!' said Randy.

'Okay, grab some flashlights and let's get going,' said Jack.

'Can we trust the batteries in the flashlights?' asked Renae, looking apprehensively at the blackness of the tunnel in the distance.

'Yeah,' said Jack. 'Three flashlights will provide some redundancy and I see that they are of the modern LED type, usually good for forty hours on a single charge. We should be quite safe with them.'

Jack unlocked the metal gate blocking the tunnel and after they were all through, he locked the door behind them before they set off down the tunnel. After about a hundred meters Randy said, 'Bingo, there's a flower shop above us that did not bother to secure their WIFI.'

Jack looked back down the tunnel and said, 'Let's skip this one rather. It's too close to our entry point. I'd feel safer if we put some more distance between us and that metal door we came in.'

'We can use this hotspot to download some maps of this drainage system,' said Randy.

'Yeah, good idea,' said Jack.

Randy worked his magic and accessed Sydney Water's website and before long he had found and retrieved various maps of the storm water drain system. 'Okay, got it. We are good to go.'

They continued making their way down the old brick tunnel. Jack admired the workmanship of what must have been a slow and painstaking job of lining the tunnel with brick. It looked as if master masons had built it.

Nearly two hundred meters further they were stopped by Randy again.

'We got a pizza restaurant above us with an open WIFI I can use.' He went down on one knee, put the notebook computer on his other knee and said, 'Here we go.'

Jack knelt down next to him and helped to steady the notebook for him. After about five minutes of furious typing and various frustrated curses, Randy looked at Jack and said, 'I got the fucker without touching his GPS. His data connection is using a WIFI network at the IBIS hotel in Darling Harbor. I can hack the hotel registry and find out which room he is in.'

'Let's first disconnect from the pizza shop WIFI and find another one further down the tunnel,' said Jack.

'No, let's go back to that first WIFI hotspot,' said Renae, clearly not liking the tunnel scene. 'We have to go back to the entrance anyway don't we?'

Jack hesitated, so Renae asked, 'Are you hoping for a tunnel right into the basement of the Ibis Hotel?'

'That would be awesome but I doubt we would get that lucky. Look you're right okay. I was hoping to pop out of a manhole somewhere closer to our destination but I'm kind of making things up as we go along. I have no time to plan and research like we would for a regular ASIO operation. I know of a secluded manhole in the Chinese Gardens where we could exit unnoticed, but I'm sure it's not going to be a walk in the park to get there from here. Storm water drains are much dirtier than the tunnel we are in now. We will be filthy by the time we get out of the Chinese Gardens and will look out-of-place once we get to the public areas.'

'How were you planning to get into Crowley's room?' asked Renae.

'I don't have an iron clad plan for that yet either. I have a vague idea of using some kind of excuse, like room service or the old cliché of checking for a gas leak.'

'If we can get a maids uniform then I could pretend to be room service,' said Renae trying to be useful.

Jack nodded and said, 'My dad's theater company has many costumes and wigs we could use but I suspect that some of Crowley's goons might be watching it. If we approached from the harbor side of the wharf I could get us in.'

'Water Taxi?' asked Randy.

'Good idea,' said Jack. 'Can you check that tunnel map and see if this tunnel goes anywhere near the harbor itself?'

'Oh god...,' said Renae. 'I'm not looking forward to that. It smells worse the further in we go.'

Randy looked up from his computer map and said. 'This tunnel eventually crosses a drain which exits into Rushcutters Bay. According to this map there is a manhole in the park above it.' He looked at Renae and added, 'The good news for you is that the storm water drain part is only sixty meters long.'

'Oh joy...' said Renae sarcastically.

Jack laughed and said, 'I'm not so keen myself but all the street and traffic cameras above us are hooked into facial recognition software which right now probably has me and Randy as its highest priority. For all I know there might be a posse of Crowley goons waiting outside that door we came in.'

Jack led the way further into the tunnel system with Randy following, one hand on Jack shoulder and the other watching his computer screen. Renae, following, could not help seeing the funny side of the scene in front of her but decided not to make light of it. They walked along in this fashion for a while then Randy found another open WIFI. He and Jack repeated their earlier maneuver until Randy announced, 'Room 134.'

'Good work,' said Jack as he helped Randy to his feet.

'Wait a minute, let's use this connection to book a water taxi as well,' said Randy. He then used a VOIP application to make an Internet phone call to the taxi company. They booked a water taxi to pick them up at Rushcutters Bay in fifteen minutes, using one of Jack's emergency credit cards as payment.

They continued walking further and eventually a passageway sloped off to the left. Randy spoke up, 'We need to take this passage folks.' The passage sloped down at about twenty degrees and had steps cut into its floor, presumably to break up water flow. It joined the storm water drain after twenty meters and Renae was relieved to discover that the drain had a central water channel with a raised walkway on both sides. A stream of water trickled along the central channel. Dirty stains on the drain walls showed that the water level sometimes came almost to ceiling height. After a while, Jack slowed and stopped, playing his torch beam along the walls.

'There it is,' he said, pointing at a few metal rungs in the wall ahead of them. They made their way over to the location and Jack was first to go up.

'I'm going to need some help to lift this thing,' said Jack from the top of the ladder. Renae was quick to seize the opportunity to get to fresh air. She brushed past Randy and climbed up to give Jack a hand. It was a tight fit at the top of the ladder but neither one of them objected.

Together they pushed the manhole cover out the hole and slid it to one side. Jack cautiously pushed his head out and saw that they were in the middle of a patch of shrubs, probably planted there to conceal the manhole and reduce tampering. He climbed out and beckoned for the others to follow and they joined him crouching down in the bushes. A lot of other people were in the park having picnics and lazing around. The mood was festive in anticipation of the New Year's Eve fireworks event and a few police were walking around playing nice with the public but on the lookout for drunk and disorderly troublemakers.

Jack looked at Renae and asked, 'Got any Makeup in you bag?'

'Why, is my face dirty?' asked Renae.

'Not for you...' grumbled Jack. 'Those cops will probably be carrying pictures of me and Randy. If we wear eye liner or something similar it could be enough of a temporary disguise to get us through the crowd. We got five minutes before the taxi gets here.'

Renae took out a small Makeup kit and got to work on the two men. When she was done she smiled and said, 'You look like two gay goth boys now.'

'Oh god...' said Randy and sighed in dismay.

'Don't put you glasses back on,' said Jack to Randy. 'They are a kind of feature of yours that make you easier to spot.'

Jack waited till a group of three police had strolled by before they exited the shrubbery and walked slowly to the water's edge. A minute or two later, a bright yellow water taxi entered the small bay and the pilot began scanning the crowd for the *party of three* he was supposed to pick up.

A few other people tried to steal the taxi but he dismissed them when they failed to provide the correct name he was looking for. Soon after that he spotted Jack and company waving frantically from the water's edge.

###

Jack and Randy sat in the water taxi with their backs to the shore line while Renae sat opposite them with a big smile on her face. Their somewhat homophobic pilot had assumed that two men with face Makeup sitting next to each other had to be gay. He gave most of his attention to Renae who was clearly enjoying the predicament the men were in. Jack just stared at her with a knowing look. Revenge would be sweet... later. He decided to play along and put his arm around Randy's shoulders and held on tight as Randy fumed and squirmed to get free. An elbow to Jack's ribs eventually did the trick and the three of them had a good laugh. It was a welcome respite from the tense situation they were in.

The taxi rounded the corner by the small naval base at Garden Island and headed in the direction of the Opera House. Its journey took them within meters of the small Island known as Fort Denison and they all three looked at each other but Jack shook his head. It was very tempting to stop off at the island and dismantle the fireworks receiver on the roof of the restaurant but if Crowley's people spotted them they would probably trigger the event or perhaps they would get shot by a sniper at Garden Island.

They continued on past the Opera House. Jack would have liked to turn his head and look but they had chosen to sit with their backs to the shore to reduce the chance of recognition by police. The taxi pilot skilfully dodged around the Manly Ferry coming out of Circular Quay before going under the Harbor Bridge and turning left into Walsh Bay. Jack directed the pilot to the metal ladder at the end of pier five where he stopped and secured the water taxi against the ladder before they climbed up onto the wharf.

They waited for the taxi to depart before Jack walked over to a door at the end of the building on the wharf and unlocked it with a key on his key holder. Once they were in he punched in a code into the alarm panel and then breathed a sigh of relief.

'We made it,' said Renae.

'Lot's of nice toys here,' said Randy as he looked around the storeroom they had entered.

'Yes,' said Jack. 'There are lighting controllers, lights, plenty of electronic stuff, cables, ropes and so on. I'm sure we might find something here which might be useful.'

'Where are the costumes and wigs?' asked Renae.

'That will be upstairs,' said Jack. 'I'll show you where in a minute. I first want Randy to look around and get an idea of what techno gizmo's we have here in case we need to use any of it later.'

'I'm sure your dad will be understanding of us helping ourselves here,' said Randy.

'That depends what you are using it for,' said a loud voice behind them.

Jack spun around and said, 'Dad! What the hell are you doing here. I thought you guys were going to spend New Years in Melbourne.'

'We were but when the police came questioning us about your alleged involvement in that train bomb, we decided to stick around in case you needed support... or bail money,' said Micky.

'It was a setup,' said Randy. 'We stumbled onto something big and they tried to discredit Jack... well... actually that was after they tried to kill him.'

Just then a beautiful mature Japanese women walked into the store-room followed by another younger very attractive woman. Renae recognized her instantly. 'Jill!' she yelped, 'I love your music!' then she got a bit embarrassed and said, 'sorry, I was channeling a crazy fan for a second there.'

'It's quite okay,' said Jill. 'Perhaps Jack should make some introductions.'

'Of course,' said Jack. 'These are my two friends, Renae and Randy.' He turned to Renae and Randy then said, 'This is my farther, Mick, my mother Akiko and my twin sister, Jill'

'What the heck is going on with your face Jack?' asked Jill. 'You look like members of a New Romantic band from the eighties.'

Jack laughed and beckoned at Renae, 'It's her fault. We needed emergency disguises and this is what she came up with.'

'Actually it's pretty good,' said Jill. 'I almost don't recognize you. Your voice gave you away though. We were enjoying the view from upstairs when we heard voices down here. I told dad it sounded like you.'

'So who is trying to kill you?' asked Akiko with concern.

'We don't know all the details but it's quite serious. A group of people have put radioactive powder into the fireworks that will displayed here tonight. They plan to contaminate the entire bridge, Opera House and Botanical Gardens area. Anyone breathing that stuff into their lungs will die a painful death sometime in the next few weeks or months.'

Jack's family was stunned into silence so he continued, 'Like Randy said, we stumbled onto a thread of information that threatened to expose the plan so they blew up the train, intending to kill me. When that failed they pinned the bombing event on me, probably intending to kill me once I had been captured. We came here to try to stop them. My soon to be dead boss is holed up in the Ibis hotel, hopefully with a portable computer that we can use to stop the event with.'

'Can't you just call the police?' asked Akiko.

'My boss, Crowley, is the head of ASIO for this state, which means he has the power to tell the police what to do and who to shoot at. As far as the police are concerned, we are very dangerous criminals bent on blowing up the Opera House along with Prince William and Kate.'

'Your boss is part of this sick scheme?' asked Mick in disbelief.

'Up to his eyeballs,' said Randy. 'I think he was going to kill me earlier today when he found out I was helping Jack with intel. I was lucky to get away.'

'What if you make an anonymous phone call to the police, tell them about the radioactive stuff,' said Jill. 'Surely they will have to investigate the fireworks, especially seeing as we have royalty in the fall-out zone.'

'Jack thinks that Crowley or his people will trigger the fireworks if they suspect that the police are on to them,' said Jill.

'Maybe your boss was just upset because he thought you were helping a bomber,' said Akiko to Randy.

Jack answered for him, 'I agree that it's a very remote possibility but the trail of evidence does make him look very dirty. We will know for sure when we get into his hotel room. If he is not guilty then he will help us prevent the fireworks from going off. If he is guilty then he is going to try to trigger the fireworks prematurely the moment we enter the room. We have to be ready for that and stop it.'

'Yes of course,' said Akiko. 'We can't let this happen. What can we do to help?'

'I don't know exactly but I have formulated a vague plan which goes like this. We need to get eyes in Crowley's room so that we can get some intel. He might not be alone and he might be armed so we need to understand the situation before we plan an attack. The idea was to get Renae to dress as a maid or something similar and have her deliver some or other complementary gift to Crowley. I assume it needs to be something on a trolley so that she actually gets to go into the room and see what's in there.'

'Here's an idea,' said Jill. 'Why not phone his room, pretending to be from the kitchen. You then tell him that the hotel is giving out free steak and champagne to all the guests and you need to know how many people to cater for in his room.'

'I like that,' said Jack.

'We will need to place that call from inside the hotel,' said Randy. 'It might ring differently with an outside call.'

'I have been to the Ibis Hotel,' said Mick. 'They have phones on the reception desk that you can call room guests on. We will need to distract the receptionist so that she does not hear you pretending to be from the kitchen.'

'You wont know if he is armed though,' said Renae.

'I'll just assume that he is. We will need to take him down the moment he answers his door to receive his free meal.'

'I've got some pepper spray in my bag,' said Jill. 'You can blind him first... then take him down much more safely.'

'That's another good idea,' said Jack.

'We will also need to disable the security camera on that floor. They usually have one at the end of the passage... two if it's a long passage. I could hack in and try somin but it could take a while,' said Randy.

'Nah, let's go low tech,' said Jack. 'I know we got some balloons here and some helium. We can get two of you to stand and chat near the end of the passage, positioned so that the balloons obscure the camera the moment we spray Crowley's face. Once we are in his room you move off again. It won't look suspicious to security.'

'It's starting to sound like a plan,' said Renae.

'Okay, Randy and I will need better disguises,' said Jack. 'There must be no chance of anyone recognizing us or this plan won't work.' He looked at Renae and said, 'I think you need to become a brunette as well. You have been on TV a few times and he might recognize you.'

'Then all of you come upstairs,' said Akiko. 'We can't do it down here.'

'I'll get the balloons ready so long,' said Mick.

'Is that chicken I'm smelling from upstairs?' asked Jack. 'I just realized how bloody hungry I am.'

###

Renae, Jack and Randy were standing in front of the service elevator on the six floor of the Ibis hotel at Darling Harbor. They had successfully faked the call to Crowley and established that he was alone in the room and he was pleased to hear that he was getting a free steak dinner with champagne. Jack had then used the reception desk phone and placed a call to the kitchen for a steak sandwich and a bottle of whatever sparkling wine was available, charged to Crowley's room. They were now waiting for someone to come up from the kitchen with the room service delivery. Jill, Akiko and Mick were standing chatting further down the passage near the security camera. Jill held a bunch of helium filled balloons tied with long strings so that they floated quite high up.

The elevator doors opened and a young male bellhop walked out carrying their delivery.

Renae used her charm on him, 'Is that for room 134?' she asked with the most loving of smiles.

'Ye... yes,' stammered the enamored bellhop, completely oblivious to Jack and Randy's presence.

'It's for my uncle and we want to surprise him. Would you mind if we delivered it in your place. It would mean so much to me...', said Renae.

'Na no problem maam,' said the bellhop and handed the covered plate and bottle to her.

'I'll order some more room service later and I would love it if you delivered it personally,' said Renae ever so sweetly.

'Yes maam,' said the bellhop as he retreated back into the elevator with a glowing smile, 'Just tell them to send Brian.'

The elevator doors closed and then Jack tied a small white apron around Renae's waist to go with the black skirt and white blouse she was wearing. Her disguise was now complete and she looked like someone who might deliver food to guests. Jack walked out into the passage and stared out the window. It was the signal for Jill, Akiko and Mick to change their position slightly so that the bunch of balloons blocked the security camera's view of the passage. When they had done so, Jack nodded at Renae and Randy and then they walked towards room 134.

Jack was quite tense despite his years of martial arts training. He glanced at Renae as she walked next to him. She gave him a nervous smile. She had a brown belt in Karate and would assist Jack if Crowley somehow got the better of him. The pepper spray was concealed in her hand under the plate of food. Randy followed behind them. His main job was to investigate Crowley's portable computer and find a way to disable the fireworks event.

Renae stopped in front of the door and readied herself for her role. Jack and Randy positioned themselves to the side of the door, out of view of the peephole. Renae knocked and waited. She heard movement inside and then saw a shadow move in behind the peephole.

'Room service,' said Renae sweetly. The door latch clacked and the door began to open. Jack watched for Renae's cue. He had to wait for her to spray Crowley before he moved. The door opened further and then Renae handed the covered plate to Crowley saying, 'Here you go sir.' He took the plate with both hands and as he did so, she pulled her hand out from under the plate and sprayed him in the face before stepping aside for Jack who was already moving into the doorway.

His leg lashed out and the kick caught Crowley in his solar plexus, knocking his breath out and sending him stumbling blindly backwards, gasping for air before tripping over an aluminum box and falling to the floor. Jack was there right behind him, not giving him the slightest opportunity to try to counter the attack. He took the roll of duct tape he had in his hand and quickly secured Crowley's hands and feet. Renae and Randy shut the door behind them as they entered.

Crowley was still wheezing and gasping at Jack's feet but Jack ignored his discomfort and frisked him, finding a pistol in the pocket of Crowley's cargo shorts.

'Bingo,' said Randy, pointing at a small metal box with switches and dials. It had an unusual antenna on top of it. 'That's a Digi XTend RF modem with high gain antenna, used for encrypted machine to machine communication.'

Randy examined the notebook computer which was connected to the modem and said, 'I found the software program they use to control the fireworks display with. I'll see if I can deactivate the program.'

Jack and Renae kept watch over Crowley while Randy continued working on the notebook. After a while he said, 'It looks as if each firework location has its own sequencer which has been preprogrammed to begin at 8:00 PM with a second program beginning at 12:00 PM. I can cancel the programs from here but I need a password to get access to the up-link.'

'I'll never give you that password,' growled Crowley as he began to recover from the attack. His face was red and tears were still streaming from his eyes due to the pepper spray.

'By preprogrammed you mean the event will continue even if we shoot holes in this computer?' asked Jack.

'That's right,' said Randy. 'We need the password or we need to get to each of the sequencers and unplug them from their power sources.'

'Won't the guys from Cooper and Sons have the password?' asked Renae.

'How do we convince them that we are the good guys?' asked Jack.

Crowley began laughing so Jack gave him a light kick in the groin and asked, 'What's so bloody funny asshole?'

Crowley groaned in pain but the smile never left his face. When he had recovered enough to speak he said, 'I told them and the police that terrorists were going to try to compromise the event by claiming that radioactive material was in the fireworks. I told them it was a hoax, that we had checked all the fireworks and they should ignore all such reports.'

His smiled broadened again and he continued, 'You're fucked Jack, besides, I changed the password. They could not stop it even if they wanted to.'

'You're bluffing,' said Jack as he foot tapped Crowley in the groin again. He was trying to wear him down to a point where he could eventually coax the password out of him.

Crowley groaned again and between clenched teeth he said, 'Check the fucking log you prick.'

Jack gave Randy a questioning look so he began tapping on the notebook keyboard then after a few seconds he said, 'He's right, the log shows a password change at 5:13 PM. And no, it does not tell us what the new password is.'

Jack tapped Crowley in the groin again and asked, 'What's the new password Benny boy?'

Fresh tears of pain welled up in Crowley's eyes and his face went red. A large vein on the side of his temple swelled visibly and it looked as if he was about to throw up but he said nothing.

Jack repeated his foot tap and said, 'I can do this all night Benny, by the time they throw your ass in jail you'll be Penny, not Benny.'

Crowley seemed to pass out for a second or two then started sucking in quick gasps of air like a woman giving child-birth. He looked like he was trying to say something so Jack let him recover enough to speak.

'The... password ... is... biteme,' said Crowley between gasps of air.

Jack could not really tell if Crowley was lying so he shrugged and nodded at Randy to try it.

'It's wrong,' said Randy, 'and we got a new problem. The message here says we have two more chances to enter the correct password before it shuts down the program for 24 hours.'

'It's byteme with a Y ... not an I,' said Crowley in painful gasps. Jack did not trust him at all but it did seem like a plausible mistake. He had no other choice really. Crowley was either lying or telling the truth and there was only one way to find out. He nodded at Randy to test it again.

'Still wrong...' said Randy. 'One chance left...'

Crowley made a sickly laughing sound then managed to say, 'I'll die before I tell you.'

Jack was tempted to kick Crowley in the groin with all his might but could not bring himself to. He knew it would make no difference and he did not enjoy violence for the sake of violence. They now had no option but to go to the location of the fireworks and disable the sequencers. At least they had prevented Crowley from triggering the even prematurely but time was running out.

Jack looked at Randy and asked, 'Does that software tell us what colors are being used at the locations?'

'Yes, I already thought of that too. I gave it a quick look and I only see purple being used on the bridge and a handful on the Opera House. I guess they did not have time to make it a full-blown purple event. There's over a hundred purple mortars on the bridge but only five on the Opera House'

'We still won't make it onto the Opera House without being apprehended or shot so I think we should get onto the bridge seeing as that is where most of the radioactive material is. If we still have time after that then we can try something desperate at the Opera House.'

'Wait, I'll give you the real password if you untie me,' said Crowley.

'Sure you will,' said Jack. He bent down and stuck duct tape over Crowley's mouth then he pressed down on a nerve in Crowley's neck until he passed out.

'Help me drag him to the toilet,' said Jack. 'I want to secure him onto something solid before we leave.'

The three of them dragged pushed and shoved Crowley's limp body to the small toilet where Jack sat Crowley on the floor facing the toilet then wrapped his arms and legs around the toilet bowl and secured him like that with more duct tape. He stuffed two small wads of wet toilet paper into Crowley's ears and covered it with pieces of duct tape.

'I don't want him to hear what plans we are discussing,' said Jack to the other two. When he was satisfied that Crowley was secure he shut the toilet door and returned with the others to the small desk where Crowley's notebook was.

'Let's call up some pictures of the Harbor Bridge so that we can plan a way to get onto it with the least amount of disturbance or unwanted attention,' said Jack. 'I have done the Bridge Climb tour as a tourist but you can only access the stairs and ladders they use from the tunnel which connects to the tourists changing rooms. We need a way to get around them.'

After looking over several pictures Renae said, 'I can see several possibilities but all of them will attract attention. People who belong on the bridge will be using the official access points.' She pointed at a metal gate on the lower arch where it came out of the road deck and said, 'See that, the bridge maintenance people use that access point but it is behind a locked security gate and we have to cross a lane of traffic to get to it.'

'Yeah, if we go there we need to look like we belong there. We have to dress like bridge maintenance engineers or electricians, ... know what I mean?' asked Jack.

'Pretending to be from Cooper and Sons will probably also be okay. If they need to make last-minute adjustments then they will need bridge access,' said Randy.

'Regardless of how we dress, we still need the keys to those security gates,' said Renae.

'I have an idea,' said Jack. 'Let's check Crowley's mobile phone and see who his friends are. One of them might have keys to the bridge.'

'It's a pity we can't imitate Crowley's voice, said Randy. 'We might be able to use that to convince the Mayor that the threat is real.'

Jack looked at Randy and said, 'Even if we could imitate him I don't think the police would act until they could confirm the story by other means. They might assume he was talking under duress and send someone here to check up on him.'

Jack continued looking through Crowley's contacts then said, 'This might work. Crowley has a number labeled Bridge Climb security. We could text them and say he is sending three plain clothes security people to check a problem with the fireworks. It's his phone so the message will show as coming from him.'

'If they call back to confirm I can pretend to be his secretary,' said Renae.

'It's worth a shot, here goes,' said Jack as he began typing the text message on the phone.

'I'm not going to wait for a reply, let's get down to the Bridge Climb tourist office,' said Jack, then picking up the gun he had taken from Crowley he said, 'We may have to threaten someone at the Bridge Climb office but if it goes wrong, it could be the end of us.'

'I'm taking this notebook computer and modem with us,' said Randy. 'I might need it later.'

'Yeah, we also don't want to leave it here for someone else to do bad things with,' said Jack.

'Hold on,' said Randy. 'Won't the cops start taking shots at us when we get onto the bridge?'

'I don't think so. We are in disguise remember. We don't match the pictures they have of us and we will be dressed in those grey jump suits that the tourists wear on the bridge. But to be sure I'll send a similar text to the Sydney police chief. I saw his number in Crowley's phone as well.'

Jack used Crowley's phone again and typed a text to Police Chief Bennett advising that three of Crowley's people would be going onto the bridge to do a security inspection.

Chapter 14

Todorova watched Golakov drive away with mixed feelings. If they failed in their mission their boss in Europe would have them both killed. Perhaps they had already told Golakov to kill him later. He had to be careful.

He walked along Maquarie street for a while then through one of many entrances into the vast Royal Botanical Gardens. He walked casually along a pathway going north towards the Opera House and smiled pleasantly at the many revelers. The park was brimming with people, many of whom had been staking out their favorite spot for days in advance of tonight's fireworks. Families were grouped around picnic blankets and children could be seeing playing various ball games. The sun was setting and many people were still arriving. It was a beautiful park but its days were limited. After tonight it would be contaminated with radioactive dust from Maralinga. The trees and grass would start dying soon afterward as well as all the people who were enjoying the outing tonight. Their deaths would be slow and painful, taking several months.

Todorova adjust the rucksack on his back. It contained a builders dust mask and an aluminum briefcase. Inside the briefcase was a disassembled VSS Vintorez subsonic sniper rifle, built by the Russians and issued to their Spetsnaz units. It weighed around seven kilograms. He also carried a video camera and a fake Federal Police security card, in case he got stopped by one of the many police he saw in the park.

The crowds of people thickened visibly as he drew closer to the Opera House but the people tended to congregate in areas which had a clear view of the Harbor Bridge because that was where the main fireworks display was going to be. This meant that the wooded areas of the park were less popular because the leafy canopy blocked an otherwise clear view of the sky over the bridge. The gardens surrounding the historic Government House were closed to the public but Todorova saw that there were some people there. Probably from families who had connections to VIP's like the Mayor or the ruling Labor Party.

At the northern end of the park section he was in, there was a sandstone hill overlooking the back of the Opera House. A lot of people were squeezed on to the grassy patch on the hill but Todorova was only interested in the steep rocky section to the right of this grass patch. It was home to a group of leafy trees and prickly bushes but most importantly, it had no people in it and it provided plenty of cover for his clandestine mission.

Todorova climbed over a few of the smaller rocks then sat down on a larger rock and pretended to be preoccupied with his camera. A few of the people on the grassy area had noticed him but they quickly lost interest as they chatted loudly with their friends. He kept watch from the corners of his eyes and after several minutes of disinterest from the nearby people, he carefully moved deeper into the underbrush and then began to crawl to the steep edge until he could go no further. He now had a clear view of the back-end of the Opera House and an almost clear view of the Harbor Bridge, but his main goal was to cover the Opera House and stop anyone from sabotaging the fireworks on the roof of the building.

Golakov watched the life fade from the eyes of the woman as he held his tight grip on her throat. They had been nice blue eyes, filled with fear and confusion but now they were devoid of emotion. That thing which gave life and expressed feelings had gone away and taken Golakov's anger with it. He felt much more relaxed now. Her husband was already dead. Golakov had broken his neck once he had established that this retired couple were the only two people present in the apartment. But killing the fat grey haired man had not quenched his anger so he took his time with the woman and gazed deep into her eyes to where her spirit lived then he squeezed until that little flame inside of her was extinguished.

He walked over to the window and looked at the magnificent view of the Harbor Bridge. The only unfortunate thing was that it was nearly seven hundred meters away which would make it extremely difficult to kill Jack if he dared to show his face on that bridge. But he had limited options when it came to choosing a location.

The top arch of the Harbor Bridge was 134 meters above sea level and it was in the middle of Sydney harbor which meant it was impossible to get any closer to the center of the bridge unless you were on a boat. He also needed to be as high as possible and the apartment he was now in was on the twenty-fifth floor of a residential block on the north shore of the harbor. What had made him angry was all the cars and people he had to put up with to get here.

The drive in from Lithgow had been a trial of patience, dealing with slow drivers who were in no hurry to go anywhere. The place was full of tourists looking at all the pretty trees and mountains. *Were there no pretty trees and mountains where they came from?* wondered Golakov. Their lack of purpose was what annoyed him most. Once they had arrived in Sydney CBD it was a hundred times worse. Every available parking spot was taken and it had taken forever just to drive from there across the bridge to the north shore. He had abandoned his car a few blocks away, in the middle of a side road because there was nowhere to park it. Then he had to act nice and polite as he knocked on apartment doors in the building until he found one which was relatively empty. Most residents had invited their friends to come and share and enjoy their view of the fireworks. One apartment had been empty but he did not have the kit to pick the lock quietly and breaking the door down would just draw too much attention.

Golakov moved some chairs around until he had them positioned near the view window then he went to the bedroom and fetched the couples entire bed and placed it on the arm rests of the four chairs. He tested it to see if it was stable enough and was pleased with the result. He climbed up on to it, then lay down on the bed to check the height. It was perfect, he had a clear view of the bridge over the top of the balcony wall. He opened his rucksack and began to prepare his sniper rifle, the same model Todorova was using.

The Bridge Climb tourist office was built under two or three of the concrete arches which supported the on-ramp to the southern side of the Harbor Bridge. The Bridge Climb operators had made good use of the location to gain access to the lower support girders of the on-ramp via two human sized tunnels through the final concrete arch. The support girders, along with various other sections of the bridge, had been fitted with walkways and safety railings so that tourists could safely gain access to the wonderful views to be had from the top of the bridge.

Jack entered the reception area of the Bridge Climb office and spoke to the woman behind the desk, 'We are the security team sent by Benjamin Crowley. Can you let Bruce know that we are here please?'

'Yes, he is expecting you. I'll give him a call,' said the receptionist. She spoke to someone on the phone then said, 'Please go through to the change rooms. He will meet you there.' Even though it was a public holiday, the tour operators were still open, charging premium prices to those people who wanted bragging rights of being on the bridge on the last day of the year. However the tourists all had to be off the bridge by 7:30 PM because of the upcoming fireworks event starting at 8:00 PM.

'Hello!' said Bruce. 'I need to size you cracker heads up for your jump suits.' He looked each of them over and chose appropriately sized items from the wall racks.

'Why do we need these?' asked Randy.

'Several reasons actually,' said Bruce. 'The two most important ones are to prevent things in your pockets from falling out onto the roadway below and causing traffic accidents and injuries. The other reason is so that we can identify you as one of our flock. It shows you are authorized to be on the bridge.' He looked at Randy's rucksack and continued, 'Tourists are not allowed to take cameras and mobile phones onto the bridge but I suppose you guys don't qualify as tourists.'

Jack gestured at the rucksack and said,' Yeah we need that computer equipment to come with us so that we can run some final diagnostics on the fireworks event sequencer. The Mayor won't be impressed if something goes wrong while she is entertaining her royal guests.'

'What kind of things can go wrong?' asked Bruce.

'Heard of angry birds?' asked Jack.

Bruce laughed and said, 'Really?'

'In theory yes. We just need to do a last-minute inspection really. It can happen that a heavy bird or something carried by the wind has hit a cable and dislodged it just enough to break a circuit.' Jack hated lying to people but the truth was not going to get them anywhere.

When they were done putting on the grey jump suits they went into the next room where Bruce issued them with their safety harnesses and said, 'The law requires that a climb leader has to accompany you at all times. Seeing as you sprang this on us so last-minute like, we don't have any climb leaders available so I'm going to have to come with you.'

'Sorry about that. Normally we just rely on the radio link in the electronic equipment to tell us if anything is wrong but with Prince William being here, the Mayor absolutely insisted that we do a manual inspection,' said Randy adding to Jack's invented story.

'I'll buy you a case of beer to make up for it,' said Jack.

'Tooheys Extra Dry, and make it two cases,' said Bruce.

'Done deal,' said Jack. 'Let's shake on it.' Bruce warmed up to them a bit more. He had clearly been unimpressed by the unexpected need to babysit a few cracker heads.

When they were ready, Bruce lead them out through the tunnel onto the girder walkway under the on-ramp. They could hear cars driving past on the road deck just meters above their heads. They walked in this fashion, under the roadway for about four hundred meters before reaching the vertical ladders which would take them up above the road deck near the southern end of the bridge arch. They followed Bruce up the ladder to a platform about halfway between the road deck and the top arch and from there they walked up a metal staircase onto the top of the bridge arch.

Bruce paused at this point and said, 'Okay, I don't know where your gizmos are so one of you will need to take the lead.'

'I never get tired of this view,' said Renae as she gazed out over the bay. Behind her the sun was getting ready to go to sleep in a bed of orange and gold sheets.

Randy took over as lead as they began to climb the steep lower end of the arch. He did not know where the radio modem had been placed but suspected it would be at the top center of the bridge as that would be more efficient for cable layouts. He kept his eyes peeled though and quickly noticed that the center cross over point, between the horizontal support girders, had been fitted with pyrotechnic mortars. Bright green explosive detonator cable snaked out from there along the cross girder to a point just next to the arch walkway he was on. All he had to do was follow the green detonator cable up the arch and it would lead him to the radio modem and the sequencer.

###

Golakov lay on the bed and peered through the telescopic sights at the bridge. He had not bothered to move the two dead bodies and he actually kind of liked having them around. They were silent witnesses to his supremacy and power and it bolstered his confidence when ever he looked their way. As he watched he saw a group of four people climb up the metal staircase onto the east arch at which point he lost sight of them again. The apartment he was in was fifty meters higher than the harbor but it was still about seventy meters lower than the top arch of the bridge which meant that he could only see people on the west arch. He had to rely on Todorova to cover the east arch. He was not worried yet, there had been some tourists earlier but this was a much smaller group, perhaps they were rich capitalists who could afford to pay a premium price for being the only people on the bridge to see the sun set on new year's eve.

After a while their head and shoulders came into view at the top of the bridge arch as they began to cross over to the west arch for the decent. This group however seemed to be very interested in something located by the flag pole on the bridge.

Golakov knew that the batteries and electronic equipment which controlled the fireworks was located there. It was possible that the tour guide was just explaining something about the fireworks and they would be on their way again... but just then he saw one of them start climbing over the railing that separated the crossover walkway from the platform at the base of the flagpole. Tourists did not do that!

He lined up on one of them and squeezed the trigger. The silenced rifle made a loud click sound, like someone with strong hands snapping their fingers and the tungsten tipped bullet was sent hurtling at a relatively slow 298 meters per second towards the bridge. Golakov watched and waited and just over two seconds later, he saw a small flash of light about two inches from the top of the arch as the heavy bullet slammed into the arch. He aimed slightly higher and squeezed the trigger again.

Todorova lay on the hard, rough rock on the edge of the hill behind the Opera House. He had trained his rifle at the bridge and was alternating between scanning the bridge arch via his telescopic sights and scanning the Opera House with his naked eyes. He noticed the four people moving up the east arch and had a full view of them as they walked up the arch towards the top of the bridge. At the top they turned and three of them started crossing over towards the west arch. The other, a female stayed on the east arch and appeared to be enjoying the view of the setting sun on the Opera House. The other three paused at the center of the bridge cross over section near the flag and began pointing at the base of the flag pole.

His position was also much lower than the bridge which meant he could only see the head and shoulders of the three people on the crossover walkway. His orders were to shoot anyone who approached the flag pole platform. He waited a few seconds to see if they moved on but then he saw one of them start climbing over the railing of the walkway so he squeezed the trigger. About a second after he fired he saw the head of one of the three center people explode. He thought it was odd because he had shot at the woman and it was too soon to be his bullet. The relatively slow muzzle velocity of the rifle meant it would take over two seconds for the bullet to cover the distance to the bridge. It had to have been Golakov.

He kept watching to see where his bullet went and a second later he was rewarded as the girl appeared to scream and look down at her leg. Todorova smiled. It had been a really difficult shot and he had to make many educated guesses as to wind speed and distance correction. The woman was now bent over and clutching her calf. He squeezed the trigger again.

###

Jack followed Randy up the arch towards the top of the bridge. He had noticed that Randy was following the green detonation chords and began to feel more confident about being able to stop the event. It seemed simple now, just follow the det-chords to the box that triggered them and then unplug the sequencer and radio modem. In his mind this job was already done and he began thinking about the fireworks on the Opera House. How the heck were they going to pull that off without getting shot or arrested. There were no public tours on to the roof of the Opera House and he only knew of two ways to get up on to the roof. None of them were plausible options under the circumstances.

He took a moment to enjoy the view as they walked up the arch stairs. The setting sun was casting a beautiful golden orange glow onto the white sails of the Opera House. It also cast a similar glow onto Renae and as the breeze lifted her hair, it seemed to catch fire and create a golden aura around her head. She looked beautiful and he locked that mental picture away in his mind and marked it as extra special. He wished he had a camera but they had not come prepared for such touristy luxuries.

At the top of the arch they turned left and followed the det-chord as it snaked along beside the walkway and then led off to the right where he saw the flag platform. Attached to the platform was a large ribbed weather proof aluminum box which seemed to be the termination point of the det-chord. The box had a clear plastic panel and inside it Randy could see the red blinking light of the radio modem.

'That's it there,' said Randy as he pointed at the box. The only thing between them and the platform was the metal railing which kept the tourists off the flag platform which doubled as a platform for various bits of equipment for servicing the various needs of police, security and other interested parties. Jack helped Randy over the railing and then felt a small shock-wave go through the railing accompanied by a barely audible metallic thud to his left. He would not have picked the sound out of the background noise if he not been holding onto the metal railing and felt the small shock-wave. Something about it troubled him. He mentally did a rerun of the shock-wave and sound trying to match it up with known data and then it suddenly and chillingly made sense.

'Get down!' yelled Jack as loudly as he could. He ducked down just as a bullet ripped through Bruce's head and splattered him with blood. Bruce collapsed onto the walkway then slipped under the railing but his safety harness stopped him from falling to the road deck eighty meters below them. Jack glanced at Renae and saw with horror that she was still standing by the east arch looking out over the bay. She had not heard him shout and had not seen Bruce get shot.

Jack quickly unclipped his safety line then started sprinting towards her and repeated his call to get down. She started turning towards him then screamed as a bullet ripped through her calf. Jack covered the last two meters, grabbed her arm with one hand, unclipped her safety line with the other hand then pulled her towards the center of the bridge and lay her down on the walkway.

Randy was lying wide-eyed on the flag platform. He looked at Jack and said 'What the fuck just happened!'

'Two shooters, one east and one west,' said Jack. 'Stay low and in the center of the bridge. Stay away from the east and west ends of the bridge and that platform you are on.'

Renae had meanwhile begun painfully pulling down the lower half of her jump suit and her eyes welled up with the effort.

'It went straight through,' said Renae in a strained voice as she examined the wound. 'No major arteries hit by the look of it.'

Jack could not see her leg, The walkway was too narrow to get next to her so he said, 'We need to stop the bleeding anyway. You need to crawl under the railing onto the platform next to Randy. He's got some duct tape in his backpack and it's going to have to be your bandage until we can get you stitched up.'

He and Randy then carefully pushed and pulled Renae until she was safely on the platform next to Randy.

Jack meanwhile had begun to formulate an idea for the Opera House. When he had pulled Renae away from the east arch he had noticed a yellow flash in the bushes behind the Opera House. His instincts and experience told him it was muzzle flash from a low power rifle. Camera flashes were white and much brighter, even from that distance. The position also made sense because it was perfect for covering both the east side of the bridge and the Opera House roof. If he could get down there and get that rifle he might be able to see and shoot the radio modems off the roof of the Opera House. He checked his watch and saw that it was 7:25 PM. He had thirty-five minutes to get down off the bridge and run over to where he saw the muzzle flash.

'Randy! Can you handle things here? I need to get to the Opera House,' asked Jack.

'No problem Jack, I just need to unplug the power cable on that sequencer,' said Randy.

'What about the gunmen?' asked Renae in a worried voice.

'They can't hit a moving target from so far away, I'll be two seconds ahead of them all the time,' said Jack.

'It's suicide Jack. You won't be two seconds ahead when you get to the Opera House,' protested Renae.

'Don't worry, I plan to take that rifle away from that shooter and use it to blow holes in the electronics on the Opera House roof,' said Jack.

'It might just work Jack but there is a small chance you might end up triggering the fireworks as well,' said Randy.

'If I do nothing it will get triggered anyway. I have to try something and that's the only plan I have,' said Jack and with that he jumped up and sprinted along the horizontal walkway towards the east arch.

The shooter on the west side seemed to be more accurate so he decided to take his chances with the east side shooter behind the Opera House. He grabbed the side rail and spun round onto the east arch steps and sprinted down the arch, taking three or four steps at a time. He was no longer connected to the railing via the safety line so if he slipped or stumbled, he might end up going over the side and falling eighty meters to the road deck below.

He slowed briefly as he neared the south end of the arch, just enough so that he could grab the railing and brake his momentum and make the bend onto the lower horizontal walkway. Something tugged hard at his collar and burnt his neck but Jack kept going. When he got to the vertical ladders he gripped the outer rails and slid down the ladder like a fireman. He shot through the hole in the road deck and hit the walkway at the bottom hard then without missing a beat he sprinted the four hundred meters back to the tunnel at the Bridge Climb office.

Once inside he relaxed slightly as he sucked in air and began pulling off the grey jump suit, it would attract too much attention out on the street. He caught sight of himself in the mirror and upon seeing a red streak along his neck where he had felt the burn, he realized that a bullet had grazed him. Two inches further in and he would be dead.

Jack checked that he still had Crowley's gun in his pants pocket then he walked briskly out of the building, ignoring the receptionist who was busy talking on the phone. Once he was outside he began running again.

Jack slowed down to a brisk walk as he approached the northern tip of the Botanical gardens behind the Opera House. The pathways had been full of people walking aimlessly through the park and he was breathless from doing a running obstacle course requiring him to run and dodge through a never-ending mass of people as well as jump over those who were lying on the grass. Fortunately the sun had slipped below the horizon and it was relatively dark which helped to obscure his frantic actions from patrolling police. He pushed past small gatherings of people who had taken to selfishly standing on the walkway, blocking the way for everyone. Now and then an alcohol fueled tough guy shouted a challenge at him for bumping them but he ignored all such small-minded distractions and continued on.

He reached the bushy outcrop from where he had seen the muzzle flash and carefully stepped into the shrubbery. The din from the endlessly talking crowds of people helped to drown out any sound he was making. As he neared the edge he crouched down and took out Crowley's pistol while he carefully scanned the underbrush. After a few moments he saw the feet of the shooter protruding from some shrubbery and then he saw the thick barrel of the silenced rifle. It was still pointed at the Harbor Bridge which meant that the shooter was unaware of his presence.

Jack was not going to try hand to hand combat with his opponent. It was five minutes before eight and he had to end this quickly and with no margin for error. He took off his T-shirt, made a bundle of it and held it in front of the pistol then he dove full length for where the shooters head ought to be. As he landed he felt the palm of his right hand brush against the shooter's hair which was all the confirmation he needed. He pulled the trigger, heard the muffled bang and felt the body beneath him go limp. He grabbed for the rifle in case it fell down the cliff edge and then he took aim at the Opera House roof, looking for the blinking red light of the radio modem. He had not bothered getting off the shooters body, no time to be squeamish.

As he peered through the telescopic sights he was much relieved to see a pulsing red glow against the side wall of the central groove on the roof. It had to be coming from the modem but the darkness made it difficult to see exactly where the modem was. He had no option other than to fire at the darkness next to the red glow. He could not see the modem box but logically, it had to be there.

The red glow continued pulsing so he adjusted his aim slightly and fired again. Still no change. On the sixth attempt the light went off and stayed off. Jack knew that it was no guarantee of success. The modem only relayed information to the sequencer and it was the sequencer that did the actual task of firing the det-chords. *Had any of his bullets hit the sequencer?* he wondered. He had no idea.

He shifted his aim to the other roof section and looked for, then located, the red pulsing glow which gave him a rough idea of where the modem was. He fired but this time nothing happened. He cocked the rifle and tried again. Still nothing. *Out of ammunition?* thought Jack. He unclipped the cartridge and ran his finger over the top. No bullets! Surely the shooter must have brought more than one cartridge. He felt around through the underbrush near him and found the rucksack and briefcase which had contained the rifle. He felt around Inside it and found another cartridge but when he ran his finger over the top he realized it was also empty. He was definitely out of ammunition. *Now what?*

###

Randy helped Renae to bind the wound in her calf with duct tape then he shifted his attention to the metal box containing the electronics for the fireworks. He opened the lid and saw a neatly arranged setup of cables and equipment. The sequencer was quite a big piece of equipment which also contained a series of switches and delay dials which allowed operators to manually create an event program.

He did not unplug the power but instead he opened his ruck sack, took out his computer and connected it to the radio modem in the box.

'What ya doing?' asked Renae.

'I had an idea a while ago while we were climbing the bridge. When Crowley changed the password, it got sent via the radio modem to the sequencer in this box where it got set and stored as the new password. I'm going to try to recover it,' said Randy.

'I thought that the radio link encrypted it,' said Renae.

'It did, but it got decrypted again on this side and I'll bet that the decrypted password is stored in this sequencer. I just need to hack into it.'

'So once you have the password you can use Crowley's computer to stop the sequencers on the Opera House?' asked Renae.

'I hope so. I can't make any promises. You can help me out a bit as well. Take my notebook computer and get it ready for internet access. I'm going to need to download some manuals and other info for this sequencer.'

'I thought your notebook only had WIFI,' said Renae.

'Correct, I can plug-in a USB modem but I don't have one seeing as my iPad can act as a WIFI hotspot.'

'Okay but there's probably still some people trying to trace your iPad signature,' said Renae.

'Yeah I know but they won't be able to get to us up here before 8:00 PM and after that it won't matter...'

Randy, assisted by Renae, worked as quickly as he could to get to know the inner working of the sequencer. It used an embedded Linux operating system which he was familiar with but it was still a slow process of downloading the required hacking tools then uploading it to the sequencer operating system and typing in terminal commands to access the features he needed. At 7:56 PM he suddenly shouted, 'Got it!' He quickly typed the password into Crowley's computer and was granted access to the radio communication system.

'Who hoo,' said Renae.

It took another precious few minutes to find and send the cancel signal to all the fireworks receivers.

'I hoped that worked but to be safe I'm going to unplug this fucking sequencer,' said Randy as he crawled back to the modem box. He reached in and switched off the power switch on the sequencer then unplugged the power cable to make doubly sure that nothing could trigger the sequencer.

'Now we wait and see,' said Renae as she checked her watch. 'Fifteen seconds till 8:00 PM.'

Chapter 15

Jack put on the dust mask he had found in the shooter's rucksack and waited. Nothing happened. He checked his watch and saw that it was 8:00 PM. After a while the nearby crowds started protesting loudly and becoming restless.

'Where's the fucking fireworks!' yelled a nearby voice.

'Yeah, light those bloody candles or we'll do it ourselves,' said another.

Someone started chanting, 'We want fireworks, we want fireworks.' More people joined in the chant and the more violently inclined young men were starting to get aggressive. By 8:15 PM a few fights had broken out and many people were starting to leave as they sensed an ugly change in the mood.

Jack took off the dust-mask then used Crowley's phone to dial Police Chief Bennett.

'Crowley! I hope you got good news. We got fights breaking out all over town,' said Bennett.

'Crowley has been arrested,' said Jack. 'We had to stop the fireworks event because the threat about radioactive dust in the fireworks is real. You need to send someone onto the bridge with a Geiger counter and check for yourself.'

'What... Who is this?' asked Bennett.

'Meet me on the grassy patch behind the Opera House and I'll show you the evidence,' said Jack. 'Also bring a body bag and some extra police to move the public away.' He ended the call. He knew that the other shooter was still out there somewhere and might be heading for the bridge to manually trigger the fireworks. He needed to get the police involved and get them to secure that bridge as soon as possible.

About ten minutes later he heard the first of the policemen starting to tell the crowd to clear off the grassy patch. After thirty minutes there were about twenty police who had succeeded in moving the crowd off the grassy patch and then Bennett pushed through onto the grass.

'Anyone seen that guy I'm supposed to meet?' asked Bennett at no one in particular.

Jack stood up quietly and said, 'Over here.'

Several flashlights probed into the underbrush and illuminated Jack as he stood muscular and bare-chested looking a lot like Bruce Lee after a fight with dried blood on his neck and chest. The unexpected sight stunned everyone into silence and no one said anything for a while then a few police pulled out their fire arms and pointed it at him.

'It's that guy who bombed the train!' said one of them.

The crowd behind the police started to murmur as they spread the news. Someone yelled, 'Kill him!'

'I'm not armed and I did not bomb the train,' said Jack loudly then he pointed at his feet and said,' This dead guy and his mate did that. Crowley was part of it too. You need to secure this area as well as the Opera House and the Bridge.' He looked directly at Bennett and spoke more quietly saying, 'That hoax Crowley told you about is not a hoax, it's very real but I and my friends have managed to stop it for now. You need to make sure that no one else gets to those fireworks and sets them off. All these people will get sick and die if you fail.'

'Put yer fucking hands up,' yelled a nearby thick-necked policeman. Jack hated the occasional dim-witted type of person who joined police and military groups just so that they could bully others around.

'I'm surrendering myself to chief Bennett, but only after he confirms what I told him,' said Jack staying motionless. He looked at Bennett again and said, 'Chief Bennett, I'm an ASIO agent with many years experience. This dead terrorist at my feet has a buddy who is at this very instant heading for the Harbor Bridge to manually set off those fireworks. You can very quickly confirm what I'm telling you by sending someone with a Geiger counter to go check. You need to send men there ASAP and stop that other terrorist. I have now warned you in front of many witnesses.'

Bennett realized he was in a fix. If Jack was correct and he ignored him, it would end his career. He eyed Jack carefully trying to sum him up then he took out his phone and made some calls. Some of the policemen near the chief overheard enough of his conversation to figure out what the threat was about and they began to look uneasy.

'There's five on each main roof of the Opera House as well,' said Jack. 'It might be quicker to get confirmation by sending a climber up there.'

'How many on the bridge?' asked Bennett.

'Over a hundred...', said Jack.

Bennett almost choked and went pale. 'Jack, if you're fucking with me I'm going to have someone shoot you while trying to escape, know what I mean?'

'I'm not fucking with you,' said Jack solemnly.

Bennett made some more phone calls then said, 'Okay, I've shut down all traffic onto the bridge and posted two cars on each end. My test guy is in a police chopper which will take him to the top of the bridge.'

They waited in silence and five minutes later a police chopper flew by and went towards the Harbor Bridge where it hovered at a position about midway up the arch. After a few seconds it lifted off and began circling the bridge. Several minutes later Bennett received a phone call then looked at Jack and said, 'Confirmed, but I'll still need to take you into custody until we have cleared this up.'

'Agreed,' said Jack and then he walked out with his hands behind his head.

By 8:05 PM Golakov was busy packing up his rifle. He knew he had shot one of the four people but then they had ducked down out of sight and he had not seen any further movement and could not see what they were doing. Obviously they had managed to disable the sequencer and now he had to go up there and do it manually. His dust mask would keep the deadly particles out of his lungs but there was still a lesser risk of his skin absorbing some of the dust particles which settled on him from the fall out. He did not have a Hazmat suit and did not have time to get one but he had to try to trigger the fireworks or his boss would have him killed. He was really angry again.

He looked down at the woman he had strangled and tried to recall the moment her life left her. It had calmed him then but it was not working now. He kicked her in the face, his ankle boot catching her jaw and breaking it off so that it hung open and skew, only supported by the skin and flesh. It made him feel a bit better but he wanted more, the need to punish was still strong with him.

He found some candles under the kitchen sink and stuck one partially down the throat of the dead woman so that only a few inches were left sticking out, then he lit the candle. He went back to the kitchen and opened the gas on all four plates of the gas stove then he shut the balcony doors and any other open windows he could find. When he was satisfied that everything was prepared correctly, he left and shut the door behind him and began to feel better as he imagined what the coming explosion would look like.

Four young girls were driving up Blues Point Road when a large man stepped out in front of them and pointed a pistol at the driver.

'Get out,' said Golakov. 'All of you out!'

The girls screamed and poured out of the car. 'Can I get my bag?' asked the blond driver.

Golakov hit her in the face with his fist and said, 'No!... bitch.'

There were many people out and about and some had stopped and stared in disbelief but he ignored them and drove off up the hill and made his way through North

Sydney and then joined the Bradfield Highway which would take him back down onto the road deck of the bridge. Once again the busy new year's eve traffic had slowed everything down to a crawl at times. As he approached the spot where the lower arch curved up out of the road deck he slammed on the brakes and screeched to a halt. He climbed up onto the side rail then onto the outer edge of the lower arch and made his way past the double set of spikes by means of hanging onto the lower sections by his finger tips and moving hand over hand till he had cleared the spikes. After that it was a simple matter of swinging his legs up onto the lower arch and pulling himself up. A simple matter for him that is.

He heard police sirens and noticed that the traffic on the bridge was diminishing rapidly. He had arrived just in time, they were closing off the bridge. Golakov was unfamiliar with the bridge but he knew he needed to get onto the upper arch but did not know where the various ladders and stairs were located. He recalled that the tourists were all climbing up via a staircase on the south side but he was on the north side. *Surely there had to be ladders and stairs this side too?* he thought. He looked around but it was difficult to see much. The bridge had rows of spotlights along the side, pointed upwards to illuminate the vertical girders and the under side of the arches. It was nice for the tourists but it was blinding for anyone standing on the lower arch.

Golakov did his best to shield his eyes from the glare and started climbing the arch stairs towards the center of the bridge. When he got there he looked around again but still did not see any ladders. He did notice that the vertical girders were supported by angled girders and he could easily climb up the angled girders, but he could not see clearly enough to tell if there were enough hand holds to make it from the top of the angled girder onto the top arch.

A helicopter approached and hovered above the top arch of the bridge for several seconds before moving off and circling the bridge. He could not see what they were doing up there but he assumed they had off loaded some policemen to guard the fireworks. He though it over and decided it was still achievable. The helicopter could not have brought more than four policemen, maybe six at a squeeze but no more than that. They would spread out over the bridge which meant he only had to deal with them one at a time, six times. Golakov screwed a silencer onto his pistol then waited for the helicopter to move to the opposite side of the bridge before he began climbing the girder. He got about halfway up before the helicopter returned so he moved around to the inside of the bridge and straddled the girder between his arms and legs. Only his hands and feet would be visible to anyone with a keen eye in the helicopter and only if they looked directly at the spot where he was.

The helicopter spotlight played over the girders around him but they did not see him. He began climbing again as soon as they moved away towards the south side of the bridge. *He had to do something about that helicopter.* Once he was on top of the upper arch there would be nowhere to hide and they probably knew that.

The last part of his girder climb was really tricky, forcing him to stretch to his full height so that he could reach past a smooth metal plate to the lower lip of the upper girder. He hung by his finger tips behind the girder while the helicopter circled around past him again then he swung his legs up first then pulled his hips up onto the ten inch lip of the girder. He now had his back to the inside of the bridge and needed to turn around if he hoped to defend himself from any attackers. He reached his right arm up and gripped the top edge of the upper arch and carefully pulled himself onto one knee and peeped over the top arch. There was no one there. He turned his heard and scanned the opposite arch looking for enemies... then he saw one.

About a hundred meters to his south he could see movement on one of the cross girders but he had to look through the bottom of the arch to see it because of the curvature. It was too far for an accurate pistol shot so he was going to need his rifle but it was packed away behind him in his rucksack. He would have to climb up onto the arch to assemble it which meant he would be an easy target for the helicopter.

Golakov waited for the helicopter to come around again then took aim at the pilot. It was only fifty meters away, an easy shot and the bullet caught the pilot in the shoulder. The pilot instinctively pulled the helicopter away from the bridge and headed for a helipad on the roof of a building in the CBD area. He was in too much pain to do much else. Golakov climbed onto the arch and lay flat as he began to assemble the sniper rifle. When he was done he took aim through the cross girders and fired. He could only see his target's lower legs but it was good enough. The bullet tore through the man's shin bone and he let out a scream as he fell off the girder and swung back and forth on a long safety line.

Golakov was not satisfied, the man was wounded but still alive. He took aim again.

Renae and Randy saw the police helicopter approaching from the south side of the bridge and lost sight of it as it descended about one hundred meters south of them then it came back into view when it ascended again after a few seconds. The curvature of the arch prevented them from seeing what was going on during those missing seconds.

Renae looked at Randy and asked, 'What's that all about?'

'Beats me,' said Randy. 'They might be sending someone to check why the fireworks never went off.'

'That's quite a risk considering those two shooters out there,' said Renae.

'I'm quite positive that Jack took care of the one on the east side. It's the other one we need to worry about,' said Randy.

'You think he's still watching the bridge?' asked Renae.

'I don't think so, unless he's got nothing better to do. He would have noticed that the fireworks are dead so there's no real reason to try to stop us anymore,' said Randy.

'Unless he decides to come here and fix it,' said Renae.

Randy gave her a worried look and said, 'Don't joke. I really hope they aren't that desperate. At least we got a police chopper circling the bridge.'

'It's weird that they seem to be ignoring us,' said Renae.

'Their attention seems to be on the lower parts of the bridge,' said Randy. 'Also, we are in a bit of a blind spot here. Those spotlights lighting up the Ausie flag above us are casting quite a dark shadow down here on the platform. They won't see us unless they actually shine their spotlight here.'

They watched in silence as the helicopter circled for a while then Renae heard a distinct *choep* sound. The helicopter immediately veered off and flew south.

Renae put her hand over Randy's mouth to stop him from saying anything, then she whispered in his ear, 'I think I heard something from over there, I'm gonna slide over and take a look.' She moved off without waiting for a reply.

Her calf throbbed quite a bit but she had bound it quite firmly with the duct tape. She felt confident that she could hobble along quite well if necessary. She slid under the walkway railing onto the crossover walkway and looked down along the arches. Too her surprise she saw a large man laying on his stomach on the inner edge of the arch. He appeared to have his attention focused on the part of the bridge where the helicopter had descended and he was busy assembling a rifle with a rather thick barrel. *He's going to shoot someone,* thought Renae. *I have to stop him.*

She also noticed the absence of road traffic on the road deck far below her. *The police must have blocked it off*, thought Renae. She slipped off her sneakers and began walking on all fours with her bum in the air, ready to fall flat on her stomach if he looked her way. Her calf hurt enough to make her eyes water but she kept going. When she got to the arch she lay flat and rested for a second then heard the heavy *snap* of the rifle as it fired followed by a scream from further down the bridge.

Oh my God, he's shooting already, thought Renae. She raised her head and saw that he was looking at a man swinging back and forth on a safety line between the two arches. He dropped his head and took aim through the rifle again.

It's now or never, thought Renae. *He'll be coming for us next.* She pushed herself up and took the last few steps to where the man lay then she swung her legs around and kicked as hard as she could with her good leg. The blow caught him on the hip and was hard enough to push his hips clear off the arch. He let go of his rifle and grabbed at the lip of the arch but his body momentum pulled him past the edge and he disappeared from view. Renae crawled to the edge and looked down, expecting to see his body falling towards the road deck but she only saw his rifle then heard it clatter faintly against the road deck. *What the hell!* thought Renae. It was not possible. She crawled to the outer side of the arch and looked down at the dark harbor water just in time to see a white splash break the surface. It was a long way down but there was enough ambient light to see the disturbance on the water. Something quite big had definitely hit the water.

Chapter 16

'Jack, I just got word that someone shot and wounded the pilot of that chopper I sent to the bridge. What do you know about that?' asked Bennett.

'My guess is that it would be the west shooter. Two snipers were taking shots at us on the bridge, from both the east and the west side of the bridge,' said Jack. They had taken him into one of the actors change rooms inside the Opera House. The crowd outside had caught hold of the rumor that he was the train bomber and wanted him dead. They were also blaming him for the failed fireworks event and wanted to kill him for that as well. It had therefore been impossible to extract Jack via the Royal Botanical Gardens due to the angry mob, so Bennett had taken him under armed escort down the stairs into the Opera House.

'Who is we?' asked Bennett.

'There were four of us,' said Jack. 'The climb leader from Bridge Climb Tours, Bruce, was killed by a head shot from the west sniper. Renae Thomson was shot in the calf...'

'Hold on, would that be the Renae Thomson who did the TV interview after she helped with rescuing people from that train bomb?'

'Yes, I tracked her down after Crowley framed me because I needed to review the film footage she had shot. She has been very helpful in solving this case.'

'And the other person?' asked Bennett.

'That would be Randy, his my ASIO intel guy and IT expert. He found a way to stop those fireworks at the last second it seems. I left him and Renae behind on the bridge when I went after that east sniper. I wanted to get his rifle and shoot the electronics on the Opera House to stop those fireworks from going off. I got one, I'm assuming Randy got the other stopped somehow.'

'Any idea where that west sniper was located?' asked Bennett.

'My guess would be somewhere in Blues Point or McMahons Point,' said Jack.

Bennett looked thoughtful for a moment then said, 'It might be connected to the explosion and fire we had on the top floor of Blues Point Tower just after 8:00 PM.'

Jack sat up straight and looked at Bennett, then said, 'That's sounds like him cleaning up after himself. How soon after that was your pilot shot?'

'About fifteen or twenty minutes after,' said Bennett.

'Shit!... he's on the bridge! You have to send men there right away. My friends are in danger!' said Jack.

Bennett's phone rang. He answered, frowned then looked at Jack and said to the caller, 'Yes, Jack is okay, he's sitting right here in front of me... okay... you sure?... okay... Can you walk?... okay I'll send help.'

Jack looked questioningly at Bennett then Bennett spoke up, 'That was Renae. She said that the sniper shot one of my men in the leg and he needs medical attention. She also said that she kicked the sniper off the bridge and he landed in the water.'

Jack was relieved and impressed. He watched Bennett make several phone calls to dispatch a medical rescue helicopter to the top of the bridge and he also sent police boats to search the water and shoreline for the sniper's body. Bennett did not think that anyone would survive a fall like that but Jack had his doubts.

Just then the door opened and in walked Sydney's Mayor. Jack was still bare-chested and bloody, sitting in a chair with his hands cuffed behind his back. She looked at him with anger and disgust then spoke to Bennett, 'Is this man responsible for killing my New Years Eve event?'

'Actually it looks more like he just saved us from an international shit storm,' said Bennett. 'We just confirmed that there is radioactive dust in your fireworks. It would have turned the entire area into a ghost town for the next fifty years and probably have killed almost a million people, including William and Kate.'

The Mayor was stunned into silence. She looked fearful and in shock. Bennett's phone rang again, he spoke briefly and issued some orders then said to the Mayor, 'We got fights and riots breaking out on both sides of the harbor. People are wanting their fireworks and they have seen all the police activity around the bridge. There have been reports of people seeing someone falling off the top of the bridge. Some people are panicking and running, causing further injuries. It's turning into a nightmare.'

'It's going to get worse if the main event at midnight is also a no-show. We need to get William and Kate away from here,' said the Mayor.

'With respect Mayor, as far as we know, only the purple fireworks have the radioactive dust contamination. It might be possible to use what's left to put on some kind of show for the people. We got three hours till midnight,' said Jack.

'It's too risky,' said Bennett. 'If even one of the contaminated fireworks gets fired it's still going to cause a major problem.'

'I agree it's a risk but if you send a bunch of people up there with radiation detection equipment and have them cut the det-chords of all the contaminated devices then it should be manageable. You will have to act fast though, clocks ticking to midnight,' said Jack.

'We need to consider it,' said the Mayor. 'The whole world watches our midnight event and it will make international news if it fails. Imagine all the awkward question we would need to answer. As a country it would be embarrassing if they find out what really happened. How the hell did it get this far anyway Bennett?'

'It's you call Mayor,' said Bennett. 'You outrank me.'

I'm not making that decision either,' said the Mayor. 'I'm calling the president. Julia can take the fall if it goes wrong.'

Jack and his family, along with Renae, Randy, chief Bennett, the Mayor and a few other VIP's sat in the Bennelong restaurant in the Opera House with views overlooking the harbor area. The Mayor had expressed her gratitude at Jack's efforts and sacrifices by inviting him and his friends and family for a late dinner prepared by the famous chef, Guillaume Brahimi. They had all had an amuse-bouche of duck fois gras, sandwiched between two discs of gingerbread. The soft rich creaminess of the fois gras was a perfect match to the slight sweetness of the gingerbread. The main meal had been just as fantastic, especially for Jack for had eaten rather poorly the entire week.

Renae had received a few stitches to her calf but had refused hospital treatment. William and Kate, at the urging of the Mayor, had returned to their hotel to watch the fireworks from the penthouse suite.

'Are we going to get our fireworks tonight?' asked the Mayor.

'My men have checked and cut the det-chords to all the contaminated fireworks and Cooper and Sons have managed to reprogram all the sequencers to give us something pretty with what's left,' said Bennett.

'Your ass is on the line if anything purple shows up in the sky,' said the Mayor.

'Thank you maam,' said Bennett.

'I'm sure it will be okay maam, by cutting those det-chords and reprogramming the sequencers to not use the purple fireworks, we have double protection from any disasters,' said Randy.

'It's a good thing you managed to extract Crowley's new password,' said Jack. 'I thought for sure we were screwed when I ran out of ammo trying to shoot that sequencer on the roof above us.'

'Actually you did totally scrap the one you shot at. I saw Cooper's guys hoisting a new one up there on a rope,' said Randy.

'What's going to happen to Crowley?' asked Jill.

'We going to bury him,' said Bennett. 'We were taking him to the paddy wagon when someone threw a knife from the crowd.' Bennett pointed to the back of his neck and said, 'It went in here and cut clean through the bone. He was dead when he hit the ground.'

'Did you see who it was?' asked Renae suspiciously.

'No, nobody saw anything. These people are like fucking ghosts,' said Bennett angrily, then realizing the Mayor and other VIP's were listening he said, 'Sorry maam...'

'I still don't know how that sniper managed to avoid falling onto the road deck on the bridge. There was another entire traffic lane between him and the water,' said Renae.

'I think he got lucky and managed to grab the lower lip of the arch girder,' said Jack. 'His body weight would have swung him under the arch girder and out towards the water then if he had enough momentum, he would have made it past the road deck into the water.'

'But surely the impact would have killed him anyway?' asked Renae. 'It's one hundred and thirty-four meters to the water from where he fell.'

'Fell? You kicked his ass off the bridge!' said Randy. 'You were awesome.'

Renae blushed a little and said, 'Oh I got lucky, his attention was focused elsewhere.'

Jack gave her hand a squeeze and said, 'I think, unless we see his body, that we should assume he survived.'

'We recovered his rifle off the road deck,' said Bennett. 'Hopefully we can get finger prints from it.'

'I hope so too but I was close enough to him to see that he was wearing black gloves,' said Renae.

'That's unfortunate...' said Jack. 'He's one tough bastard. I really hope he died because the world can do without people like him.'

'So we got nothing to go with, no idea who they were working for and what the agenda was,' said Randy.

'Well we got that shooter behind the Opera House,' said Jack. 'It might give us something to work with.'

'It's time,' said the Mayor. Everyone got up and went outside onto the huge balcony. There was a countdown and then the fireworks display erupted. It was quite an impressive show with the highlight being a waterfall of white sparkles which seemingly flowed off the bridge road deck into the harbor water below while a set of white streamers shot high into the air whilst being pock-marked by smaller explosions of color to resemble a peacock's tail. The VIP's, the crowds along the harbor and the millions of TV viewers all enjoyed the display but those in the know were tense. The fear of purple was strong but much to their relief, it turned out well. No purple explosions were seen in the sky.

'Happy new year everyone,' said Jack. He gave everyone a hug and once they had all expressed their good wishes for the new year, he and Renae slipped away quietly. He was not going to sleep on her couch tonight.

The End